GRAVE WARS

JANE LADLING MYSTERY SERIES
BOOK SIX

GENA SHOWALTER
JILL MONROE

AUTHOR TALK MEDIA LLC

Cover Created by Leni Kauffman

Editing by AZ Editing

Proofreading by Naomi Lane

Chapter Header by kytalpa through Depositphotos.com

Ornamental Breaks by CRStocker through CreativeFabrica.com

Usually we dedicate our latest book to our families, but for this book...it's to ourselves!

※ ※ ※ ※

Special thanks goes to Naomi Lane. The Songbirds, Falconcrests. Eagleshields and Skyhawks of our Patreon and Mandy M. Roth who is always there for us!

CHAPTER ONE

Thou shall not sneak into the home of an opposing candidate, even if the door is unlocked.

–Jane Ladling's Campaign Companion Code

"I think there's something wrong with my flyer." Jane Ladling paused in the middle of the neighborhood sidewalk, frowning at the stack of political flyers in her gloved hands.

Cold wind blew, flapping the pages. The sun shone at full wattage, illuminating the brilliant design—if she did say so herself. However, the beams provided zero heat, allowing the niggle in her mind to keep her frozen in place. What was she missing?

"Looks amazing to me, and I should know," said the darling woman at Jane's right. Fiona Lawrence had just celebrated sixty-three years on this Earth, so, yes, she'd obviously seen enough advertisements to qualify as an expert judge. "Critiquing other people's work is my superpower."

Jane wasn't one to doubt her best friend. And the flyer

1

was amazing. But… Her frown deepened as she read the text more closely. Cupcakes with Conrad Ryan. Hosted by Jane Ladling. Located at Garden of Memories. February 29th. 12:00-2:00.

Lovely font. An invitation to get to know the new resident ready to serve as the world's most amazing sheriff. Adorable photo of the usually stoic Conrad smiling. A glorious expression exclusively reserved for Jane. Something she hated to share. Alas. Anything to help the precious man live his dream.

"I love the hugeness of his last name," Fiona said with something akin to amusement hiding in her tone.

Had Jane made **RYAN** large enough to cover two lines? Yes. How else was the name supposed to stand out to the good people of Aurelian Hills, Georgia? A small town big in gold, community, and lately, murder. The very reason a special election for sheriff was so urgent. Conrad versus Joshua "Josh" Gunn, a well-respected deputy who'd served her hometown for over fifteen years.

Too bad for Gunn, no better lawman existed than Conrad, Jane's on-again boyfriend. In the past six months, the smoking hot former special agent had helped her solve a string of homicides. Oh, he might have done the "official" legwork, but Jane had unofficially created theories, questioned mountains of suspects, and provided delicious snacks. Though she owned and operated a landlocked cemetery, she wasn't exaggerating or bragging when she said she had an incomparable knack for investigating and solving the most complex of crimes; Jane was simply being honest. But making flyers… where had she gone wrong?

She traced a blunt-tipped nail over the text. His name. Hers. The cemetery's. Hmm. Her gaze zoomed back to her name in particular. Jane Ladling…Ryan. She gasped as a light dawned, the problem suddenly glaringly obvious. *Oh. My. Gosh*. Once seen, there was no unseeing it.

"No, no, no," she groaned, hugging the stack to her chest. She rocked from heel to toe in embarrassment. Then she looked at the horror again. No matter what she did—blink, shake her head, will the text to change—the abomination remained the same.

How could she have done this? How had she missed this travesty of an error when she proofed the flyer not once or twice but three times? The way she'd positioned their names... Her stomach rolled. It looked as if she and Conrad had gotten married, and this was how they'd decided to announce it.

"Found the problem, did you?" Fiona asked. Oh yeah. Jane definitely detected amusement.

"Just great! You see it too." Cheeks heating despite the chill, Jane tapped the paper, pointing to the worst mistake anyone anywhere had ever made in the history of forever. "Be honest. Does it seem like I'm announcing a change in my marital status?"

A smile bloomed over the older woman's beautiful face. "Are you worried Conrad will think you did it on purpose? As a hint?"

"No! Definitely not." But maybe? She unleashed the groan brewing at the back of her throat. The guy knew and accepted her refusal to wed. That she was willing to date him was a miracle. And her recent softening toward the idea of love? The biggest miracle of all. But marriage? Never!

The women in her family were cursed. *Fall in love and lose the guy. Marry him and watch him die*. Although, yes, Jane had recently admitted the curse might possibly be self-inflicted. The reason she'd agreed to finally get serious with her favorite lawman. Like a big girl, she'd decided to stop cheating on her future with her past and running away.

Still, she'd be eternally mortified if he saw this flyer. "I think it goes without saying that we'll be removing and burning all evidence of my blunder." Jane whipped out her phone. "I'll text Beau and tell him to retrace his steps, reclaim every paper he's hung or passed out, then meet us at the hearse."

She'd parked the family car at the entrance of The Treasure Trove, the largest neighborhood in Aurelian Hills. From there, she and Fiona had gone right. Beauregard "Beau" Harden, a war vet and her dearest childhood friend, went left with his military bud, Trick. The two darlings had volunteered to help...after demanding payment in the form of casseroles.

"Wait." Fiona pointed to a tree-lined residential street. "There's Beau. He's headed straight for us, and he's got a stack of flyers under his arm. Think he noticed the totally accidental and not at all subconscious error?"

Please no.

Fiona made a funny noise. "Oh, wow. Tiffany replaced Trick."

"Trick is irreplaceable." A one-of-a-kind computer whiz. But Beau, a wildly attractive blond giant did in fact walk beside Tiffany Hotchkins, Jane's nemesis. The elegant brunette looked adorable in a dusty rose knit cap topped with a white and silver pom pom.

Beau said something to the widow, and Tiffany laughed while batting at his arm.

What in the everloving *what*? Were they flirting with each other? Jane swallowed the sour taste in her mouth and marched toward them, determined to end... whatever this was. The last two men romantically linked to Tiffany had ended up dead or in jail. A fate *not* happening to Beau, thank you.

The other woman spotted her and waved a flyer as she

approached. "Inquiring minds want to know. Did you marry Agent Ryan in secret?"

Gah! Having a nemesis sucked. They always gloried in your mishaps. She and Tiffany had clashed in elementary school, and things had only grown worse from there. Didn't help that Jane was the one who'd discovered the widow's philandering husband's dead body. Or that she'd later connected Tiffany's fiancé to a murder, exposing the scandal to the whole town.

"No, I most certainly did not," Jane said in a snippy tone. "Anyone who suggests these handbills say otherwise is being ridiculous."

"What happened to Trick?" Fiona asked Beau, cutting off any further suggestions of marriage. "He requested a chicken pot pie casserole as soon as we returned to Jane's cottage."

"Got a call for a job." The vet's delivery held a note of apology, but his expression hinted at glee. "I'll eat his portion of the casserole, don't you worry. Not one bite will go to waste."

Beau owned Peach State Security, and Trick handled all the tech stuff. "Will Tiffany be joining us for lunch?" Jane pushed the words past gritted teeth.

"Oh, yes. Where he goes, I go," Tiffany answered. Flashing an over-bright smile, she linked her arm through his. "I hired Beau as my bodyguard today. Just in case you were wondering."

Hmm. According to gossip Jane heard inadvertently, the Widow Hots was broke and desperate for money. When she put her family estate on the market, she'd only added fuel to the rumors. So how could she afford Beau's services?

"Where is Conrad, anyway?" Tiffany asked, glancing around.

"That is a private matter I won't discuss." Because Jane didn't know! He'd recently moved into a charming craftsman bungalow only minutes from her home. They called each other every morning and met up at least once a day. Today he'd texted instead.

> Running some errands. I'll explain later. Maybe. Before your brilliant mind cooks up twenty different scenarios about what I'm doing, I'll admit it involves a surprise for you.

What surprise? Finding out had been her next task after the campaign leaflet distribution, which must be put on hold now. "Since the flyers are missing a period after my last name —which is a perfectly natural grammatical error," Jane rushed to add, "we're going to gather–"

"Oops." Tiffany winced as at least fifty of her flyers fluttered away in the wind. The papers—went—everywhere. "I'm sorry," she said, and yes, okay, she did sound remorseful. "It wasn't on purpose, I promise."

With a humph, Jane gave chase, the soles of her winter boots thumping against concrete and grass. She snatched every paper to cross her path while Fiona, Beau and Tiffany grabbed the others.

Oh! There! One determined page flew just out of reach, up the porch steps of a ranch style home, ending its journey trapped against a door.

Realization punched her. Uh-oh.

Jane drew up short. This was no ordinary house; it belonged to Josh Gunn. The competition. She'd avoided the property only minutes ago. No sense rubbing his upcoming loss in his face.

She stared at the single-story modest abode shaped in an L and painted a rich caramel. The sage green door remained closed. No movement in either of the large windows flanking it.

Was a hidden camera recording her every move? More

and more people were installing those these days. She knew because *she* had one, thanks to Conrad and Beau. Would she wake up tomorrow to discover Deputy Gunn had given the feed to Ashley Katz at *The Headliner*, the town's most hopping message board and weekly publication. The reporter had it out for Jane.

She could already imagine the article title. *Cemetery Girl Six Feet Deep in Sabotage!*

A panting Tiffany halted at her side, breath misting in front of her face. "Why are you staring at the door?"

Jane shook her head, jolting from her thoughts and into the present. "Let's grab the flyer and go." She reached out and—

Tiffany clasped her arm, stopping her. "Look. While we're alone, I'd like to talk to you about something." A mix of dread and entreaty etched her expression, and Jane stiffened. "I've given this a lot of thought, and I believe it might be fun for me to, um, move in. To the Garden. Of Memories. With you. I can learn more about the cemetery and my relatives."

Ah. Okay. Things suddenly made sense. The rumors about the widow's finances must be true. She needed a place to live and was desperate enough to spend precious funds to gain Beau's company. The only way to arrange a true face-to-face with Jane.

"First, you nicknamed me Cemetery Girl as a kid and convinced our fellow students I'm too weird to befriend. Now you wish to live among the dead? Why would you ever think I'd say yes? Second, we aren't family."

"First," the beautiful brunette echoed, squaring her shoulders, "*you* are the one who convinced the kids of your weirdness. Not me. Second, we share a great-grandfather. How is that not a blood relation?"

Gah! Truth was truth, and there was no way around it. But. "A so-called blood relation doesn't make a family."

7

Neither of Jane's parents had wanted her. Her dad fled before she was born and phoned her every so often when he remembered her existence. Her mom shipped her to Pops and Grandma Lily one summer and never came for her.

Jane and Pops used to work puzzles together and watch mysteries. Lily taught her how to cook and garden. Losing them one after the other still hurt. They'd left a gaping hole in Jane's heart. But a family of her own making had helped patch it. Fiona and her boyfriend, the retiring Sheriff Raymond Moore. Conrad, Beau and Trick, plus their other buds, Holden and Isaac. And, of course, the glue that held everyone in place, Rolex, the world's most perfect guard cat.

"You only want to move in so you can search for gold." The widow wasn't the only victim of the rumor mill. Too many townspeople believed an old caretaker at the cemetery had buried his loot in coffins.

Jane had to deal with gold hunters sneaking about, digging up graves and destroying her pristine grounds. And yes, okay, having a roommate help out *would* be nice. Just not Tiff. Anyone but Tiff.

"Think it over. Please." The other woman raised her chin. "Obviously, I don't know how to fight the Ladling curse. Maybe you can, and I'm just spit balling here, help me."

She sighed. Tiffany wasn't lying about the curse. A dead husband and incarcerated fiancé were the proof in the pudding. "How is it you think I can help you?"

"Considering your relationship with Conrad, you've become an expert at overlooking looming doom. If I can do the same, maybe I can be happy again."

Jane ground her teeth. "We aren't doomed." Granted, a familiar fear attempted to resurge at times, but dang it, she trusted Conrad to stick. At Christmas, she'd promised him a chance to demonstrate it.

Want different results, do something different.

The widow soldiered on, slipping right past the denial. "Plus, I can be a huge benefit to Conrad's campaign. Watch and see." She pasted a fake smile on her face and knocked on the door. "I'll convince whoever lives here to vote for your boyfriend."

"The competition lives here," Jane squealed, two ideas battling to the death inside her mind. Run vs Stay. In the end, stay won. She attempted to cobble together an excuse to offer the deputy. *Hi, sir. We're voting for Conrad in the coming election, but we're trespassing on your private property for a good reason—heart health.* The heart health of the town.

"My bad," Tiffany said, paling. "Should we bail?"

"Of course not. We'll appear guilty of something." Stomach churning, she glanced over her shoulder. Fiona and Beau still hustled about, gathering papers. So, Jane did it. She knocked with more force than her companion. "Let me do the talking."

Wait. The deputy's door swung open, hinges creaking, revealing—huh. An empty foyer.

A burning, metallic scent wafted from inside. Jane frowned as an unwelcome sensation slithered down her spine. "Deputy Gunn?" she called, remaining in the entryway while scanning the inside of his house.

Nothing seemed out of place. Everything was clean. Above a side table, two holes broke the smooth eggshell white wall. The plaster edges appeared singed. Beyond that, six large manila folders formed a line across the carpet, as if placed there on purpose. An equal number of purple envelopes were stacked on the coffee table. A sleek, black camera with a pop-up flash and rubberized eyepiece rested on a leather couch, the LCD screen active. Almost looked like a behind-the-scenes sting operation in action.

Then Jane spied an unmoving leg. "Deputy Gunn!" She rushed inside in case he required aid, only to come to an abrupt stop. A groan parted her lips. Crimson wet a gash on the side of his head. His eyes stared faraway, his features relaxed. An expression she knew all too well. But maybe... maybe he was just dazed?

Jane swallowed and examined the rest of him. He lay on his back, one arm outstretched, the other propped on his stomach. His legs were bent at the knees, as if he'd attempted to curl into a fetal ball but lacked the strength. A shattered mug lay at his side, the liquid contents wetting his buzz cut. He wore a white T-shirt, worn jeans and socks. She'd seen him around town, but he looked much older than his fifty-something years, as if he'd aged a decade in a matter of weeks.

Her gaze zoomed back to his chest. No sign of life.

No, he wasn't dazed.

"What?" Tiffany said, bumping into her. She gasped and pressed a trembling hand over her mouth. "Is that a...?"

"Yes, that's a dead body," Jane confirmed. "We need to call 911."

CHAPTER TWO

Thou shall always be prepared to use a fake British accent
and pretend to be a strategist if the situation calls for it.

–Jane Ladling's Campaign Companion Code

*J*ane sat in a conference room at the police station. Alone. Upon Sheriff Moore's directive, an officer had escorted her in here. Fiona, Beau and Tiffany had joined her at some point, only to be questioned individually and released. When two of the trio demanded to remain with her—guess who asked for an escort home—an order to vacate followed.

What was going on? Why was Jane being singled out? She'd been here five hours, possibly an entire year. And yes, she'd scoped out several locations to hang new campaign posters. Agents from the Georgia Bureau of Homicide had flown in and out of the room, armed with questions:

How long have you known Mr. Gunn?

Have you ever mailed or delivered letters to him?

GENA SHOWALTER & JILL MONROE

Did you speak with the deputy during one of your unofficial investigations?

They suspected her of committing the crime, didn't they? Jane bit the inside of her lip. This wasn't her first interrogation, so she knew the drill. She should absolutely call an attorney. But goodness gracious, she preferred Conrad. He made everything better. Plus, her last lawyer had been murdered, so why risk hiring another?

If Conrad were here, he'd use his unwavering determination and unmistakable authority to remind her that no one with any sort of intelligence would consider her a murder suspect. Sure, she had motive, flimsy though it may be. Some could even say she had killed to take out her boyfriend's only competition. But she also had a rock solid alibi, thank you. She'd spent the entire morning with Fiona, Beau and Trick, driving to neighborhoods to hang those flyers. No doubt a hundred home security systems could verify this.

But what if the agents thought she'd hired a hitman?

Her stomach churned. Political scandals always involved hitmen, right? And what was the time of death anyway? Maybe they believed she'd killed the deputy earlier to "conveniently" find him later. Though, as a woman who'd stumbled across not one, but four corpses in less than a year, there was nothing convenient about the experience.

The door handle twisted, and Conrad burst into the conference room, a tower of strength. His black hair was a mess, as if he'd plowed his fingers through the strands repeatedly. Tension etched his features, his electric baby blues bright with concern. "Another body, Jane? Really?"

Oh, thank goodness! She shot to her feet. He opened his arms, and she nearly leaped over the table to fall into his embrace. As she nuzzled against his cashmere sweater, getting as close as humanly possible, his warmth enfolded her, bringing the scent of dry cedar and exotic spices.

"The good news is, the body wasn't on my property this time," she said. "That's progress."

He pulled back just enough to cup her cheeks and peer into her eyes. "Are you okay?"

Was she? As the owner of a cemetery, she wasn't unaccustomed to death. But discovering the body of Deputy Joshua Gunn was different. More personal because he'd been in his own home, where he must have felt safest. "I am," she decided. Now. "Do you know what's going on?"

"Sheriff Moore briefed me as much as he was able." Conrad's mouth flattened into a grim line. "He has questions for us. Apparently, Deputy Gunn received a series of death threats and compiled folders on possible culprits. You and I are among the list of six."

Her back shot ramrod straight. "But that's preposterous!"

"Don't worry. We'll establish our innocence." He lowered his head and gave her a sweet kiss. "If necessary, we'll launch our own investigation."

Okay, maybe she shouldn't admit this, considering someone had tragically died, but excitement infiltrated her cells. Finally! She'd get to officially unofficially team up with the incomparable Conrad Ryan and show him how to properly solve a case: suspect everyone. He'd gain his first taste of Team Truth, a group of top-notch expert sleuths she spearheaded. Members included her found family.

She pursed her lips. The team might have to include Tiffany in their upcoming meeting, since she discovered the body with Jane. But this was a one time invitation only, and that was that.

"Once we're successful," she said, practically bouncing in her winter boots, "we can start our own private investigator firm. Ryan and Ladling." Honestly, it should be Ladling and Ryan, as she'd been the one to solve all those other cases, but Grandma Lily taught her proper etiquette. Others first.

A hint of amusement played at the edge of his expression. "Or Ryan and Ladling-Ryan?"

Her breath lodged in her throat. Oh dang. Was he suggesting... A flush scorched her face. Yeah, he was. "You noticed my mistake on the flyer."

"I did. I'm surprised you didn't." He bobbed his head from side to side. "Until it was too late, of course."

Hmm. What was he trying to say? What did he think of the error? His tone revealed nothing.

A knock sounded on the door, saving her from having to whip up an intelligent response.

Silver-bearded Sheriff Moore didn't wait for permission to enter but made his way inside, carrying a mug of—hmm, not regular coffee, black, as usual. Tea, maybe? Did Jane detect notes of chamomile and lavender? After suffering a massive heart attack three months ago, he must be making dietary changes to aid his recovery, on top of his impending retirement. Almost all of it thanks to Fiona, no doubt.

Displaying his usual gruffness, he met Jane's gaze and nodded. An assurance everything was gonna be alright? Or a sucks to be you condolence?

A special agent with salt-and-pepper hair trailed him, a thick file in hand. Oh! Tim Barrow, Conrad's former partner. The father of three wore his GBH uniform—blue collared shirt and khakis—and appeared just as grim as the sheriff.

"Oi," she muttered. This couldn't be good.

Barrow shook Conrad's hand, then offered Jane as he sat at the other side of the conference table. Sheriff Moore perched beside him, sipping that tea.

"Hello, Jane," Barrow said.

"Hello, guvner." Oh no she did not just use a British accent.

The agent shook away his confusion. "Sorry it took a murder to bring me back to Aurelian Hills."

"Me too," Conrad replied, holding out a chair for Jane. As she eased down, he claimed the spot next to her. They joined hands under the table. His palm was dry and his fingers steady; he wasn't the least bit nervous, and the knowledge fortified her calm. Yes, Conrad was better than any lawyer. "So, it *is* a murder."

"Looks that way," Barrow announced with a tired sigh. "The security system was disabled from the inside a little before eight this morning. The coroner believes the deputy died approximately an hour before Jane and Ms. Hotchkins discovered him."

That meant he was murdered at roughly 9:30, prior to her arrival in his neighborhood. Yes! Fully alibied for once.

A lingering knot between her shoulders loosened a fraction. But still. Poor Josh Gunn.

"We've confirmed your whereabouts at that time," the sheriff added. "Barring any new evidence to the contrary, you're both in the clear. So, I reminded Special Agent Barrow about your familiarity with the town and citizens, Conrad. Not to mention you'll be running in a few months. He agreed to share what we found. We'd appreciate your input on the case. Yours too, Jane."

Well. That explained why they'd kept her in this room for so long. They required her assistance. Triumph and vindication flooded her. *Deputy Gunn, I vow to find your killer and bring them to justice as swiftly as possible.*

"How did he die?" Jane asked, getting down to business.

Barrow's face turned grim. "Drug overdose. We don't think he did it to himself. The substance was most likely mixed into his coffee. We're waiting on more tests results to confirm."

Oh. "I just assumed…" her words trailed.

"What did you assume, Jane?" Conrad asked, confirmation that he trusted her process.

"I saw bullet holes in his wall and smelled gunpowder. There was a gash on his head. He wasn't shot or beaten?"

Barrow shuffled through a stack of photos and slid one across the table. The victim. "He fell and hit his head on the coffee table." The agent eased over another photo. The wall with the bullet holes. "Two shots were fired inside Gunn's home, though none struck him. We've questioned his neighbors, but none heard the blasts."

Sheriff Moore swallowed heavily. "Either the shooter used a suppressor, or the shots happened days, weeks or months ago. Or both. He'd grown paranoid lately. Thought someone was following him all the time. We looked into it, but found no evidence of a stalker. I admit, I figured he was exaggerating."

To her, Deputy Gunn was a familiar face in town. For Conrad, competition. But to the sheriff, Josh Gunn had been a member of his team. Someone he hired, trained and cared for.

Conrad tapped his fingers on the tabletop. "Why didn't Deputy Gunn report the shots if they happened before his murder? Is there a chance he fired his own weapon?"

Excellent questions.

"The holes came from a forty-caliber pistol," Barrow said. "Not his police-issued gun or anything registered to him."

So...why kill someone with something as unpredictable as drugs when you had a perfectly good silenced gun you'd proven you weren't afraid to use?

The agent slid a series of other photos their way. "As I shared with you a bit ago, the deputy received threats in purple envelopes. He put together a file on the six individuals he suspected. We aren't sure if other files were taken by the perpetrator."

She remembered spotting those purple envelopes before spying the body. Jane leaned forward and peered at the names on Josh Gunn's list. Took her a while, but she finally managed to decipher her and Conrad's names in the deputy's messy scrawl.

Sheriff Moore took another sip of his tea and placed his mug on the table. "Before you ask, the others include his neighbor Hugh Garfield, reporter Ashley Katz, bartender Thomas Bennett, and an alleged crime boss Josh referred to only as the Gentleman."

Barrow flicked the man an irritated glance, as if he'd said too much. Interesting. The agent hoped to hide details from a former colleague.

The sheriff shrugged, all *what are you going to do, fire me?*

Jane examined each photo and frowned. Oh, wow. The perpetrator used magazine cutouts to spell different messages. Old school, and very creepy.

> Drop out or bleed
> You aren't wanted here
> Enjoy your final days
> Your a dead man
> You can't hide

"Well, whoever did the deed needs an immediate grammar lesson. Seeing that travesty of language actually hurts me inside, and I'm insulted anyone considered me the culprit, even for a second," Jane stated. "I mean, really. *Your* a dead man? Without an apostrophe R E? And as you can clearly see, those threats lack any kind of pizzazz. Had I sent him anything, I would have used glitter glue and fabric swatches and threatened to fish out his organs with a knitting needle."

Conrad rubbed his free hand over his mouth, as if masking a laugh. "Since you're asking us for help, it's safe to say Gunn's files supplied no real evidence against us."

"That's correct. We believe his only reason for including you both centered around his fear of losing the election. However, there *is* credible evidence pointing to some of the others." The sheriff lifted a cautionary finger. "Don't forget, we aren't sure if other files exist. The killer could have taken them on the way out."

"I'm going to proceed as if they didn't. For now." Jane would concentrate on the known persons of interest.

She let different scenarios roll through her mind. What if there were two perpetrators? One with a gun, one with drugs. The two could have worked together or separately.

Or, what if a single perpetrator used the gunshots to send investigators down a rabbit hole, wasting time and resources? What if the shots happened first but failed to hit their target, so the killer snuck in the drugs?

Her frown returned. The sheriff mentioned a bartender as a fellow purple envelope suspect. Intoxication could explain missing a man and hitting a wall, right?

To start her interrogations with him or Ashley Katz, the *Headliner* reporter?

During the previous murder investigation, Ashley had shown herself to be combative and willing to cross any line to develop a story. Plus, she tended to use all caps when sending texts, a sure sign of a cold, withered heart.

"What was his rationale for suspecting Ms. Katz?" she asked.

"Greed," Sheriff Moore said. "The deputy claimed she printed a fake story about him planting drugs on Thomas Bennett, the bartender, in order to arrest him. Josh hired a lawyer and was putting together a lawsuit to sue her for millions."

Jane remembered the article in question. The journalist had shredded Deputy Gunn's character, which had been deserved if true. But how better to get out from under a lawsuit than murder?

She tapped her chin, thoughtful. "Well? Did the deputy abuse his power?"

"Not to my knowledge." Lines furrowed across the older man's brow. "We brought in an outside oversight team to pour through his files and speak to anyone who'd issued a complaint against him in the past three years. The investigators found no hard evidence to fully substantiate the reporter's story, and she never gave up her source."

No "hard" evidence? Did they find soft evidence then? And who was this mysterious source? Thomas Bennett himself?

"The oversight team spoke with Bennett, who Josh arrested for drug possession," Sheriff Moore continued. "In the file, he—Josh—mentioned using Bennett as his CI. Apparently the bartender secretly works for an emerging mobster known as, you guessed it, the Gentleman, and Josh hoped to identify other members of the gang."

Hmm. So Deputy Gunn could have been a threat to their lucrative, most likely illegal enterprises. "I've never heard of this mobster. Is he or she based in Aurelian Hills?"

"Supposedly. We know little else about the Gentleman," Barrow said, being his usual diplomatic self and telling her nothing.

Perhaps Deputy Gunn got too close to the truth, and this Gentleman person ordered a hit. That would explain the suppressor. Hitmen used those, right?

But again, a mobster? A hitman? In Aurelian Hills? Well, why not? Mr. Bennett and the Gentleman took the top two spots on Jane's suspect list, respectively, pushing Ms. Katz to number three. With the caveat that she'd move up or down the moment Jane learned more about that soft evidence, of course.

"Why is the neighbor a person of interest?" Conrad asked.

"They were arguing about a tree," Barrow explained, offering no more details.

A neighborly dispute gone bad? Mr. Garfield joined Ms. Katz on tier three.

With Mr. Bennett and the Gentleman remaining at the top of the list, she took a closer look at those crime scene photos, searching for anything a hired killer might have left behind: gloves, lock-picking tools, a fake mustache.

She blinked in confusion. "What in the world is that?" She pointed to a weird blob near the body.

The sheriff's nose wrinkled. "Yeah, we found a pile of hair, most strands from a different source. We're having them analyzed."

A variety of hair types? Did that mean a group of people had watched as the killer did his—or her—thing?

Conrad leaned back in his seat. "So how can we help?"

Sheriff Moore waved to Barrow, who sighed and said, "Thanks to our previous investigations, I know how uncooperative, secretive and downright misleading many of the citizens of Aurelian Hills can be. No offense," he added with a wince at Jane. "You are now considered a resident, Conrad, and I'll get further with you at my side. Considering the magnitude and scope of the case, the boss gave me permission to use you as a special consultant."

Happiness for Conrad and disappointment for herself rained over Jane. In his speech, Barrow had singled out Conrad on purpose, ensuring there was no misunderstanding about whom he wished to hire. Did she understand the agent's reasoning? Yes. But also mostly no. In only a few minutes, she'd put the list of four in the perfect order. Bennett, the Gentleman, Katz/Garfield. Who else could say the same?

Conrad gave a firm nod. "I'm in—on one condition. Give

me permission to confer with *my* consultant throughout the case. Her name is Jane Ladling, and she's very good at solving mysteries."

Sheriff Moore pinched the bridge of his nose, and Special Agent Barrow mimicked Conrad's pose, leaning back in his chair and crossing his arms over his chest.

"We figured you'd say that," the agent admitted. "There may be certain details we don't want you sharing." His dark gaze zoomed to Jane. "Sorry," he muttered before refocusing on Conrad. "But. You'll be allowed to confer with her about anything else."

Hey, it was better than their previous arrangement where he told her nothing.

Conrad gave her hand a comforting squeeze. "Any interest in being *my* consultant, Jane?"

"Honestly? You can't afford my rates," she replied—and she meant it. The first down payment involved never mentioning the flyer from heck again. "But yes. Okay. We'll work out an installment plan." And she would do what she always did. Solve the case with style.

"I'm in," he repeated with a nod. "But first, there's something I need to do."

CHAPTER THREE

Thou shall practice your best "supportive girlfriend" smile
for photo ops, even if your face hurts from grinning.

–Jane Ladling's Campaign Companion Code

*J*ane parked in the gravel driveway, sliding her
hearse between Fiona's sporty red convertible
and Beau's old, battered truck with a cab full of
luggage. Going somewhere? After their release, the amazing
duo had worked together to get her treasured family vehicle
to the police station.

She didn't emerge right away. Feeling as if she'd been
overseas for decades, she took a moment to breathe deep and
drank in the sight of her childhood home. Jane refused to call
the cottage weathered, preferring the word 'cozy' instead.
Sure, the blue shutters cried out for a fresh coat of paint, but
nothing beat the wraparound porch, perfect for knitting or
sipping sweet tea any day of the year. Even today, as winter
attempted to ward off spring. The crocuses already dazzled

with delicate purple and yellow flowers. Just like that, she was invigorated.

When Conrad parked his shiny black SUV, she killed the engine and entered the chill. He'd name the vehicle Jel, which just happened to be her initials. A fact she thrilled over every time she spotted the car. But why had he refused to aid GBH right away? What must he do?

The beautiful former agent strode to her side and together they climbed the porch steps. As they neared the door, he clasped Jane's hand and spun her around to face him.

Her heartbeat accelerated as her gaze met his. "Are you going to command me not to launch my own investigation?" Was that his important errand?

"As if you'd follow any orders. Sweetheart, this isn't my first day as your almost husband." A smile teased the corner of his mouth when she sputtered. "I'm returning to the station. I just wanted to make sure you got home okay."

Ohhh. How sweet. He was, without a doubt, the world's best boyfriend. Jane reached up to toy with the ends of his hair, the strands a little longer since he'd left the Bureau. "Will you come back for dinner?"

"Nothing can stop me." He leaned in and kissed her. "One more thing. You plan to interview the bartender. I see it in your eyes. Do me a favor and give Barrow a few days to question the guy before you approach him. If you insist on speaking with someone today, and we both know you will, start with the neighbor. But do not leave this cottage without Beau. Understand? In fact, keep him by your side for the rest of the day. I'll return around seven." He lowered his chin, his intense gaze mesmerizing her. "Now, this next part is most important." His voice dipped, growing husky. "Are your listening ears on?"

"When you use that tone," she replied with a shiver, "always."

Blue eyes glittering, he told her, "I'd like you to pack a bag, scoop up your murderous cat, and move in with me."

Jane sucked air between her teeth. "I didn't hear you. My listening ears fell off."

"Temporarily if you prefer," he added as if she hadn't spoken.

There was just so much to unpack. First, he knew her too well. Of course she wanted to interview the bartender right away. She intended to learn more about illicit activities committed with or without the Gentleman. Did Conrad think she would spook the guy, jeopardizing the case?

Well, he might not be wrong. So fine. Whatever. She could concentrate on the neighbor and his dispute with the deputy, as requested. Because how easy it would've been for Mr. Garfield to sneak into the house, disable the security system, and add drugs to the coffee grounds? But what did Conrad mean by "move in with me?" For how long exactly? The tacked on "temporarily if you prefer" hung between them heavier than a fall fog.

Despite the cold, sweat beaded on her nape. She couldn't...they shouldn't...he wouldn't... He understood how seriously she took her role as caretaker of the Garden. How she never wished to leave. But *she* understood Conrad was smack dab in the middle of renovating the home he'd just bought; making him return to her guest bedroom would only delay his work. And yeah, she kind of wanted to see him swing a hammer.

Still, she wrestled with indecision. Yes or no? Stay or go? On one hand, this was the best time to leave the Garden. On the other, she'd be moving in with Conrad, and while they'd already done the whole "live together" thing once before while he'd searched for a place of his own, this scenario felt different. They'd been broken up then, and they were very much a couple now. So...

Yes or no? Stay or go?

Conrad took mercy on her struggle to form a coherent response. "If Gunn was right and there's some kind of wanna be mobster in Aurelian Hills, I want you protected nonstop. Bonus, you'll get to help me decorate my new place."

Though she tried to resist temptation, a wave of anticipation and excitement swept through her, erasing every possible reason to refuse. What would a temporary move-in hurt? They fit like puzzle pieces. And honestly, she desperately missed having him and his adorable corgi Cheddar around.

Besides, who wouldn't want to decorate his amazing craftsman bungalow? She remembered his sterile condo in Atlanta. All whites and beiges with no personal touch. The poor darling! Could she really allow her favorite person on Earth to live in such a prison? But dang it, she didn't have to be so happy about this. The curse...

Argh! She wasn't traveling that road again. The curse could suck it. Never again would she permit fear to make her decisions and ruin her life.

"Alright," she grumbled. "I'll move in with you temporarily. On two conditions. We pretend the flyer nonsense never happened. And I have unlimited veto power for your furnishings."

"Unlimited veto power, yes. But the flyer? Sorry, sweetheart." He tapped a finger to his temple. "It's already immortalized. It can never die."

"This is one murder I'm happy to commit." Wait. A suspicion arose. She licked her lips. "Are you, um, doing this because you hope to get, um, married someday?" Would she break his big, beautiful heart with her refusal? Were they

GENA SHOWALTER & JILL MONROE

destined to split over this issue? Because put him in peril? Hardly. She wasn't a monster.

"I am not," he said, almost amused.

Double argh! The curse was working overtime today. She'd have to be more selective with her thought processes. "I accept your terms, I guess. Just know I'll exact revenge every time you remind me of the flyer."

"I expect no less from my campaign manager. You are my favorite brat, after all."

The affection in his voice left her smiling. "What about Tiffany Hotchkins? She found the body with me. Is she in danger?"

"Not unless she pulls a Jane and launches an investigation of her own." He winked at her. "Be safe, sweetheart." With that, he rapped his knuckles against the door twice. Then he kissed her lips, winked again, and strode off.

Smile widening, Jane placed a hand on her fluttery stomach, turned and entered the house only to halt as astonishment punched her. Platters of food covered her coffee table. Cheese straws, fried green tomatoes, deviled eggs, fried okra, pimento cheese bites, sausage balls and sweet pecan pralines.

Fiona sat in her usual floral print chair. Beau perched on one end of the couch...and Tiffany perched on the other, petting Rolex. Her cat allowed someone other than Jane to pet him? Were pigs flying, too?

The darling feline lay curled up in the socialite's lap, making biscuits and purring. But, but... kneading those sweet little paws into a selected nap spot was reserved for Jane and Jane alone. She beat back a spark of hurt. It was good for Rolex to make new friends. Just...why did said new friend have to be her childhood tormentor?

"Jane!" Fiona sprang from her chair and hurried over to gather her close. A mother hen who'd stumbled upon a missing chick. "Are you okay? Tell me everything!"

Jane sucked up the comfort like a sponge. How she loved and adored this precious woman. "I'm good. Truly."

They clung to each other as her dearest friend led her to the coffee table and urged her to eat. Should she snag the seat between Beau and Tiff or take the recliner? Oh, what the heck. Jane plopped herself between the vet and the widow.

"The food is divine," Tiffany said. "I helped Fiona whip everything together. Obviously my talents are boundless."

What! The widow had the audacity to help Jane's Fiona? Such nerve!

The grandmother prepared and passed over a plate of goodies as Jane conveyed what she'd learned at the station, omitting names–for now. Share everything with a non-Team Truth member? No.

"I'll do some digging on *the Headliner*," Beau said. "See what I find."

"Thank you."

"A bona fide mobster? Here?" Fiona shook her head with disappointment. "No one has breathed a word of this to me."

"Probably because your ears are too sweet for such sour talk." Tiffany nuzzled her cheek against Rolex's soft fur.

The adorable traitor closed his eyes in bliss. Would he come to Jane if she called?

Instead of finding out, she leveled a steady glare on the beautiful socialite. "Let's forget the mobster angle for a sec." Something was beginning to bother her about the widow's unexpected appearance now that the situation was crystal clear. "I'm wondering why you decided to hire Beau today of all days. Did you know we planned to take flyers to Deputy Gunn's neighborhood? Did you tag along so you could kill him and use us as an alibi?"

Tiffany glared at her. "I knew you'd find a way to blame me! What reason could I possibly have? I never even met the man. Except when he gave me a speeding ticket. Which I didn't deserve, incidentally. I was only going fifteen miles per hour over the limit!"

"I think everyone can agree you're right about the ticket," Jane said, "but you do have a reason. A big one. Huge. After all, Deputy Gunn worked the case for your late husband and imprisoned fiancé. He could have discovered something terrible about you. Was he blackmailing you, so you decided to off him?"

"You'd enjoy that, wouldn't you?" The widow hugged Rolex closer. And he let her. "You're always nice to everyone but me, your only remaining family in Aurelian Hills."

She surged to her feet. "Hey! I'm not the bad guy here. I'm not the one who disturbed a perfectly preserved grave on a hunt for gold. As if I'm too foolish to realize you hope to set up shop on the premises so you can hunt again."

Beau choked on his tea. "Never disturbed a grave while searching for gold, Jane? Really?"

Okay yes, she may have unearthed a coffin in the middle of the night, on the hunt for nuggets, but she'd done it for justice. What better, more noble motive? And yeah, she might have insisted Beau help her. But justice trumped greed. So why did guilt prick her and the urge to apologize bloom?

"Fine, whatever. Forget Tiffany. She's off the suspect list —for now." But that didn't mean she was an honorary member of Team Truth. Or dishonorary for that matter.

Jane lifted her nose while easing into her seat. She bit into an admittedly delicious sausage ball and withdrew her cell. "Excuse me a moment. I must send a message and it can't wait." After devouring the rest of the sausage delicacy, she texted Beau and Fiona the names she'd omitted from her explanation. *Hugh Garfield, Thomas Bennett, Ashley Katz and the Gentleman.*

The military vet's phone dinged first. He glanced at the screen, then blinked at Jane. "These are your suspects?"

Why was his phone not on silent during an official team meeting? Wow. Guess they needed to institute some rules.

"Yes," she replied just before Fiona exclaimed, "Oh look. I just got your text, Jane!"

She swallowed a sigh. Considering her fellow team members weren't great at stealth, she might as well continue. "Any details you uncover will be greatly appreciated. But before you start, will you question the neighbor with me, Beau? I promised Conrad I wouldn't leave your side. Full disclosure, I'm pretty sure I'm supposed to use you as a human shield if danger erupts. That was my takeaway, anyway."

Beau was nodding before she finished her sentence. "You better mean it. If something happens and you *don't* use me as a shield, I will forever question our friendship."

"You guys can't be serious," Tiffany cried. "You plan on harassing the victim's neighbor, accusing him of committing the crime?"

"It's called investigating." Jane flipped her hair over one shoulder and stood once again. "But yes."

Fiona's dark eyes glittered with mirth. "You two go on and solve the case. Tiff and I will clean up our mess before we head out."

"Thank you, Fee." She humphed at Tiffany and grabbed a hat from a side table. As she positioned the lacy creation on her head, she sailed outside with Beau on her heels. "I hope you brought your A game, Bo Bo, because I'm packing heat."

He groaned. "Tell me you aren't carrying a gun before Conrad or I train you and get you licensed, Jane."

She rolled her eyes. "My heat is my skill. Obviously. So what are we waiting for? Let's do this."

* * * *

ONLY HALF AN HOUR LATER, Jane knocked on Mr. Garfield's front door. Beau stood tall at her side. Thankfully, authorities weren't stomping around inside Mr. Gunn's residence, so there was no one to discourage her.

When the owner failed to appear, she rang the doorbell. Finally, Hugh Garfield opened up. He was an older man, with thin white hair, weathered skin and what looked to be a perma-scowl. A nasal cannula plugged his nose, the clear hose leading to a portable oxygen tank.

"What?" he demanded.

Beau offered a friendly smile. "I apologize for showing up at your home without an invitation, sir, but I suggest–"

"No buts," Jane interjected, certain he planned to suggest the guy pick a new tone or else. "I apologize for showing up uninvited too," she added as her mind pieced clues together. Sneaking in and out of Mr. Gunn's house might not have been as easy for the neighbor as she'd assumed. Unless he was faking his medical condition. Or maybe he'd paid someone to do the deed? Hmm. This hitman theory was gaining traction.

Mr. Garfield humphed at the other man, making Jane regret doing the same to the widow, then he wagged a finger at her. "You're the girl who left that awful flyer. The would-be sheriff's wife."

Awful? How dare he!

Beau's snicker helped her focus-up.

"Hello," she said, flashing her brightest smile, as if she didn't have a care. "I'm Jane Ladling, the very single owner of Garden of Memories. Well, not *single* single. Conrad and I are dating. And we're super serious. Totally exclusive. But—"

"I'm not buying a casket," he suddenly spat. "Doubt I'm

voting for your boyfriend, either. We have nothing more to say to each other." He stepped back, moving to shut the door in her face.

"I don't want to sell you a casket," she rushed out. "And I'm not here to discuss whatever ridiculous reason you have for refusing to vote for the world's greatest homicide investigator. The only person able to fill Sheriff Moore's shoes and keep our streets safe. So if you want to jeopardize everyone's future, that's on you. I'm here to discuss your neighbor, Josh Gunn, and the tree you share."

Mr. Garfield paused, his scowl deepening. "You mean *my* tree. Mine." He thumped his chest for emphasis and actually shuffled onto the porch, joining her and Beau. "Josh demanded I chop her down. But how can I? She's my wife."

Uh...

Beau double-blinked. "Are you telling us you are married to a tree?"

"No. And yes." Wheezing, the old man wheeled his oxygen tank to the edge of the porch. Once he caught his breath, he waved to a Southern Red Oak, its limbs reaching skyward, the massive trunk covered with rough bark and deep grooves. "When Patty died, our kids had her ashes put in one of those degradable urns and planted here. Josh found out and said I'd turned the entire neighborhood into a cemetery, destroying property values. That Patty haunted him now."

What nonsense. Some people claimed Garden of Memories was haunted, too, but they couldn't be more wrong. There was only one (supposedly) haunted spot in Aurelian Hills, and it was the old Clayton Boarding House. The lonely, isolated shack perched atop a hill no one dared to venture unless dared.

Honestly, living in a cemetery rocked. Talk about the wealthiest place on Earth. It's been said graveyards are the richest spots in the world, filled with hopes and dreams never fulfilled, books never written, songs never sung, inventions never shared, and cures never discovered. Jane agreed. But the residents never abandoned you, happy memories collected, and peace reigned. Until dead bodies showed up where they weren't supposed to be, of course.

"Would you or your kids kill to protect Patty?" Beau asked with the finesse of a bull. To gauge Mr. Garfield's reaction?

The old man nodded. "You better believe we would."

Hold up. He'd confessed to the murder?

"But we didn't," Mr. Garfield added to her disappointment. "Why bother? He was so intolerable, I knew it was only a matter of time before someone did the job for us." He smirked. "And lookie here. They did."

What an unpleasant man. "Were you here around nine thirty this morning?"

"I sure was, and I'll tell you what I told the cops. I didn't notice anything odd. Now do me a favor and get off my property." He lumbered to the door.

"Vote Conrad Ryan for sheriff," Jane called.

The entire way to his foyer, he grumbled about the scourge of pushy women. As soon as the entrance shut behind his oxygen tank, a lock clicked.

"Well. He's definitely capable of murder, but I don't think he did it," Jane said to Beau. No way Mr. Garfield's illness was faked. And it wasn't like he could travel unnoticed with that oxygen tank. In fact, would he even risk firing a gun near that tank? "We should probably invite him to dinner. He's lonely."

Beau did another double-blink. "I doubt I will ever understand you."

"We should also speak with his kids," she continued, as if he hadn't spoken. What was there to understand? She was an open book. "But, to be honest, I'm leaning more heavily into the mobster theory."

She consulted her gut for confirmation, but...hmm. Her gut had gone silent, offering zero feedback. Why? Too busy frothing over the coming move-in with Conrad? Jane gulped, instantly drowning in nervousness. *Fight the fear!*

"I'll do that digging for info you requested," Beau said. "I'll probably start with Thomas Bennett. You and I can reconvene tomorrow morning and decide our next move."

"Perfect." She'd do some digging, too. "While we're out, I should order new campaign posters."

"There's no need. Conrad is without competition. He's guaranteed the position."

"That's the silliest thing I've ever heard. Lack of competition doesn't mean we slack off, Beauregard. Have I taught you nothing?"

He snorted. They walked to the hearse, and Beau opened the driver's door for her before hustling into the passenger seat. As she keyed the engine, he buckled up. A golden oldie spilled from the speakers. Her beloved grandfather's favorite type of song. She cranked the heater to full blast.

Once they she'd finished at the print shop, she and Beau headed to the cottage. Hey! Fiona's car was gone. Only Beau's truck remained, but his luggage no longer filling the back cab. Had one of his buds come and picked everything up?

Beau helped her out, walked her to the door, and kissed her cheek. "I'm not leaving until Conrad arrives," he said. "While you deal with what's waiting for you inside, I'll be on the grounds, checking security cameras."

"Thank you. For everything." Wait. "What's waiting for me inside?"

He merely smiled and strode off.

"Beau! What's waiting inside?"

Without looking back, he waved. A half frustrated, half

amused noise left her. Dang, she adored this guy. He was sweet, funny and unwaveringly loyal. And as soon as this case ended, she was gonna crank up her efforts to find him the perfect girlfriend.

She entered the cottage only to freeze. The luggage occupied half of her living room. Worse, Tiffany remained. Rolex wound himself between the widow's parted feet, rubbing against her calves.

Before Jane could work up a good mad, Tiff blurted out, "I have nowhere else to go. No friends. As soon as my accounts dried up, Abigail stopped answering my texts."

Abigail Waynes-Kirkland, the worst of the worst.

"Please. Fiona thinks it's a wonderful idea. She left a note." Tiffany thrust a piece of paper Jane's way.

She swiped it and read, "Bring your new roomie to my house tomorrow for dinner. I'm making my famous blueberry pancakes, and she's your golden ticket past the door."

Gah! As if Jane could really throw out the brunette now. She *lived* for those pancakes. And really, if ever there was a time for the irritating woman to stay, it was now, while Jane lived elsewhere.

"Very well. You can crash here for a few weeks. Just until you find your own place. But you must oversee the maintenance of the burial plots while I'm at Conrad's. It's temporary, so don't go getting any ideas about moving in forever. And you can't dig up anything."

Tiffany's eyes widened. "What! You're leaving me here alone? With dead people?" She drew in a deep breath before offering a brittle smile. "Never mind. It's fine. Everything is fine. Thank you for providing me with shelter. I'll be forever grateful, and I won't do any digging, I promise."

"You are welcome," she replied. Because manners. And also, Tiffany's appreciation caught her off guard. It was absolutely, beyond any doubt suspicious. Did the widow want something else? "If you'll excuse me. I have some work and packing to do." Up first, printing the story Ashley Katz wrote about Deputy Gunn. "Rolex, honey, come with momma." She strode toward the office in the back of the cottage, afraid to breathe as she waited for the most perfect black cat to give chase.

Only when he bounded her way did she relax. Despite the gruesome murder and flyer incident, this had actually turned out to be a great day. Jane had a couple solid leads, and the Garden had a guardian during her very short-term absence. No question, she would be back. Often. This land was her baby. Her family.

So why did a flame of foreboding suddenly spark deep in her heart?

CHAPTER FOUR

Thou shall always wear the perfect outfit on campaign days,
even if it means borrowing from a semi-feral roommate.

–Jane Ladling's Campaign Companion Code

*J*ane walked a leashed Rolex over the threshold of
Conrad's bungalow. The future Aurelian Hills
sheriff wasn't far behind, with her small
overnight bag hanging from his grip. She paused in the foyer,
taking everything in. Conrad's attention to detail shone
through every nook and cranny.

Once marred by scratches and water stains, the hardwood floor now radiated with a rich, lustrous glow. He'd
revived the faded hues, the warm tones revealing the natural
grain. Bending at the knee, she crouched to run her fingers
over the smooth surface. At this angle, she spotted grooves
he hadn't erased. Flaws that only added to the beauty.

He'd painted the walls a muted blue, which surprised her.
She'd expected a respectable taupe or beige and had been

prepared to flash her veto card. The powdered cornflower fit the home's past, present and future.

The only furniture came from his apartment. A TV, plus the sofa, love seat and coffee table, each with a smattering of Cheddar's fur, giving the pieces a homey feel. Carpentry tools and various equipment occupied a far corner.

"You bought a cat tree?" she asked, blinking back tears she never wanted the lawman to see. A three-tiered beauty pressed against a large bay window overlooking the front yard.

Rolex prowled over and clawed to the top. By the time she removed his leash, she'd gained control of her emotions.

"There's a litter box and feeding station in the guest bedroom," Conrad explained.

Great! The tears welled again. He was so sweet and kind.

"As you can see, the home is practically a blank canvas requiring your decorating talents."

Her heart swelled. He'd left the canvas untouched for her, hadn't he?

Only a plaque and picture hung on the wall. She moved closer for a better look. The engraving read Sheriff Conrad Ryan. Bad Guys Don't Stand a Chance. A present she'd given him at Christmas. Her chest clenched.

Her gaze slid to the picture, and she gasped. The terrible, wonderful man had actually framed the flyer.

"The map you gifted to me is hanging in my bedroom." He sidled up and slung an arm over her shoulders. "When you think up my punishment for the flyer," he said, his tone smooth, "remember I'm a typical guy. I hate snuggling on the couch while watching a movie, long conversations that end with a closer bond, and surprise feasts with our closest friends." He performed an exaggerated shudder. "Yuck."

A laugh bubbled from her. She pressed her fingers against

her mouth to smother the sound. Encouraging him was not the route she planned to go. "Where's Cheddar?"

"Spending the night with Wyatt. Rolex can learn the place without a dog trailing his every step."

Wyatt Murray. His foster brother. And goodness gracious, was there anyone more thoughtful than Conrad?

He kissed her temple. "I want this house to feel like a home to you. Promise me you won't hesitate to change anything."

"I promise," she whispered, a lump growing in her throat.

Rolex meowed loudly, grabbing their attention. The forlorn kitty stared her straight in the eye. Another mournful meow followed. As if…no. No way he missed Tiffany. He must be hungry. Yes, yes. That was it. Jane claimed her bag. "I have his food in here."

"C'mon, I washed a special bowl for him in the kitchen."

A special bowl? If ever there was a marrying man… Her chest clenched again.

Okay, time to get the conversation moving in another direction. "Are you going to knock any of these walls down?" she asked as he led her from the foyer, past the dining room and through the living area. They entered the kitchen.

"I know open concept is popular, but I prefer keeping the original architecture."

"Agreed."

He'd retained the glass knobs on the cabinets and the stained-glass inserts featuring red tomatoes and green peppers.

She traced a verdant green vine on the wallpaper with her fingertip. "And this. It's one of the reasons I fell in love with the house before you bought it."

"Same."

Conrad had refreshed the paint, restored the floors, and

replaced the laminate counter with granite. The classic lines of the cabinetry would never require updating. Other than a new stainless steel refrigerator, the ancient appliances stayed in place.

The window seat in the corner only needed hand sewn decorative pillows and–

Nope. When she decorated for him, and she would, she would pick what he liked. Not her. Because she would never live here. Never become mistress of Ryan Manor.

He crossed to the cabinet with a gorgeous artisanal tile backsplash, withdrew the bowl, and passed it to Jane. The name Rolex was scripted in the center, making it a treasure beyond price.

"You are amazing, Conrad," she offered softly.

"Am I forgiven for the flyer?"

"No," she said, and he laughed. "But I'm thrilled to tell you the design has been adjusted and fresh copies ordered."

"Too bad," he replied with a (manly) pout.

Ignoring the flutter in her veins, she prepared her darling feline's meal and steered the conversation back to the case. "Did Deputy Gunn have a reason to think he'd been marked for death? Other than those creepy letters, I mean."

Remembering when *she'd* been marked for death, she shuddered. Was Gunn followed as he'd believed? His vehicle tampered with? Strange graffiti appearing on his stuff?

"Barrow and I read notes made by the oversight investigators hired by Sheriff Moore. Gunn reported someone stole his sunglasses, motorcycle and golf clubs. He also said his back door was unlocked every morning, after he was sure to lock it each night."

Hmm. "Someone might have been toying with him."

"My thoughts exactly."

Okay, how awesome was this? Here they were, discussing

a case in the open, like any normal couple. "What did the deputy do when the investigators found no evidence of a stalker?"

"Stopped filing reports."

"Because it did him no good, or because he hoped to find the culprit on his own and exact revenge?" By filing additional reports, he would've created a much clearer legal trail, making himself a top suspect if something happened to the perpetrator.

"It's possible he went rogue, which is very on brand for the citizens of Aurelian Hills." Electric blues crackling with humor, he tweaked her nose. "You hungry?"

"Starved," she admitted. Earlier, she'd been too wrapped up in the interview and too nervous about this move-in to enjoy more than that solo sausage ball. By the time her stomach calmed, she'd been too busy deciding what to pack. With her snack cake of a boyfriend at her side, the world felt right, which frightened her. Just not enough to curb her appetite again.

He led her from the kitchen, passing by the barstools salvaged from his old apartment. They stopped at the built-in buffet in the dining room. Two plates, glasses of sweet tea and sets of silverware waited with a feast. The rich, savory scent of chicken, vegetables and spices teased her nose, but it was the yeasty aroma of freshly baked bread that truly made her mouth water.

Her pulse raced extra fast when she noted where the decadent morsels came from. "You went to Daisy's." Only Jane's most favorite diner in all the land, famous for their chicken noodle soup. The lump in her throat returned and expanded, nearly cutting off her airway.

Conrad distracted her by doling out the meal and leading her to the couch to eat. "How'd your meeting with Hugh Garfield go? As well as ours?"

Between bites and sips, she described the interaction. "He's cranky, bordering on hostile, but devoted to his wife's memory, which is kind of sweet."

"Yeah, the same as ours," Conrad confirmed.

"If it helps, I don't think he's our guy. I'm not sure he would survive a walk to and from the deputy's house to secretly dose a mug or bag of coffee grounds. But. I haven't ruled out his kids. Do you happen to know their names?"

"Ken and Barbie. And no, I'm not kidding. Speaking of children, the deputy has them, too, all adults. Two sons, Charlie and Ralph, and a daughter, Madeline. The ex-wife of eight years, who lives in California, says he's estranged from each of them."

Ohhh. New names for Jane's list. "Was the deputy romantic with anyone?"

"Denise Allen, owner of the Gilded Scissor Beauty Shop. If there were others, we haven't uncovered them yet."

Perhaps Jane should speak with the stylist ASAP. She could really use a trim. Considering she'd interviewed and cleared Denise for the last case, requesting an appointment shouldn't be *too* awkward.

Conrad gave her nose another tweak. "I can see the wheels turning in your head. Add Allen to your list if you are so inclined, but I don't think she's our killer. Barrow and I chatted with her. She dated the deputy a few months, but broke up with him two weeks ago. Said he was obsessed with uncovering the Gentleman's identity. Apparently, Gunn firmly believed he'd get a string of convictions to catapult himself to the position of sheriff, gaining the power to run me out of town."

Jane went still. "Deputy Gunn didn't like you?"

He shrugged, unconcerned, and took a drink of his sweet tea. "Believe it or not, he isn't the first."

"Well. Clearly he was a terrible judge of character. The

worst! Why, if Garden of Memories wasn't landlocked, and he'd purchased a plot, I would refund his money and turn his corpse away!"

"Thank you for defending my honor, sweetheart." The teasing note in his voice sent shivers cascading down her spine. "Barrow and his team are going through the wealth of evidence they found in the deputy's home. In the morning, he's interviewing Thomas Bennett. I'll be there, but out of sight. Since Bennett works at the Gold Star Lounge, I thought you and I could pay him a visit during his shift tomorrow evening."

A stake out? At one of the ritziest places in town? Excitement exploded like fireworks inside her. "Yes, yes, a thousand times yes." She had never rescheduled a chance to devour Fiona's blueberry pancakes, but just this once, an exception must be made for justice.

Conrad smiled at her, and she smiled back, the moment rife with affection. They finished their meal while playfully arguing about the best dipping sauces for french fries. An unfair battle between store-bought ranch and made from scratch jalapeño peach jam. Considering Jane was the final judge, the jam won.

"All right, Miss Ladling. It's time to relax. No shop talk for the rest of the evening."

"Deal."

After storing the leftovers in the fridge and washing the dishes, they returned to the living room. Together they cuddled and watched a fascinating documentary about two bestselling romance novelists who solved a string of crimes aboard a cruise ship. Rolex slept in his tree.

Jane offered her commentary, outlining different motives for every suspect—at first. Conrad was just so warm. And he smelled so good. And her eyelids were as heavy as boulders. And...

✦ ✦ ✦ ✦

THE SWEET AROMA of coffee lured Jane from the best sleep of her life. Stretching, utterly content, she blinked open her eyes. Sunlight poured through a somewhat familiar living room. But it wasn't her living room. What—why—realization dawned, and she sagged into the couch. *Conrad's bungalow.* The move in. Temporarily! Only temporarily.

At some point, Conrad put a pillow under her head and draped a blanket over her lower half. He'd also abandoned ship.

Rolex hadn't venture off, though. The little trooper perched atop the tree. Hmm. He was peering outside, reminding her of a vet who'd come home from war to find his lady love had died in his absence.

A pot clanged. Ah. Conrad must be in the kitchen, preparing breakfast. The darling man.

She checked her phone and gasped at the time. 7:23. Like, a.m., as in morning? Seriously? When had she ever slept so late? Six messages awaited her. Three from Beau, the rest from Fiona, Tiffany and, huh. Her oldest half sister June. They hadn't spoken in several years.

> June: Hi.

How was Jane supposed to respond to that? She changed her sister's text name to Juniverse, just because, then regulated the odd greeting to a back burner, to be dissected and returned later.

> Fionality: Well? How'd your first night at Conrad's go?

Jane shot her friend a swift response.

43

> Amazing! But here's something not amazing. I have to do the hardest thing ever and postpone our pancake dinner. Conrad needs me on a stakeout tonight!

> Tiffinator: I don't really have to walk around the graves, do I????????

Jane had recently changed the widow's screen name. Eyes narrowing, lips pursing, she danced her thumbs over the keyboard, typing.

> YES! Also, I need you to watch Rolex for me this evening.

Better the feline stay with someone he liked, for whatever reason, than spend the evening alone.

> Beaudyguard: I'll pick you up at 8:00 dull.

> Beaudyguard: That means I could be a few minutes late. Or early.

> Beaudyguard: You probably want to know why I'm picking you up. You hope to speak with Ashley Katz, right?

Of course Jane hoped to speak with Ashley Katz today. A fellow Gunn suspect/file. Wait. 8:00, as in a.m.? Jane scrambled to her feet, gathered the toiletries from her bag, and shut herself in the bathroom, where she brushed her teeth, showered, and dressed in a vintage inspired jersey-knit fit and flare emerald dress. Oh no, she'd accidentally packed her beret instead of the picture hat with a dramatic brim perfect for questioning a suspect. Well, there was nothing she could do about it now.

With ten minutes to spare, she checked her messages and discovered a response from Fiona.

> Fionality: A stakeout!! Oh, how exciting! Yes, we can postpone, hon. You let me know a good day, and I'll make sure there's a hot stack of blueberry pancakes waiting just for you. And Tiffany.

Joy burst through Jane as she went in search of Conrad, who hadn't left the kitchen. He was shirtless and drool-worthy, his tanned muscles on display. The most adorable tattoos sleeved his arms, each image a drawing once done by his younger brother, who'd died in a car accident, along with Conrad's mother and father.

Sweet young Conrad had spent years in the system, bouncing from home to home.

Overcome with a sudden burst of affection for him, Jane rushed over and threw her arms around his waist, pressing her cheek between his shoulder blades. He'd had a tough life, yet he wasn't allowing his past to define him. Every day, he fought for better.

He inspired her.

"What's this for?" he asked, sounding both amused and grateful as he kissed her knuckles. "Not that I'm complaining."

"You're you, and you're wonderful and perfect, and I just wanted to hug you." She sniff-sniffed. Did she detect... Heart racing, Jane peeked around him. She did! "You're preparing your ultra-famous cinnamon sugar French toast." A treat he'd only teased her with before this.

"With extra cinnamon," he said, tossing a wink over his shoulder. When he spotted her hat, his smile widened. He turned, facing her fully, a spatula in hand. "You are adorable."

A blush burned her cheeks. "Thank you. You are delicious."

"You're talking to the French toast, aren't you?" he asked with a snort, returning his focus to the food.

"Mostly."

He barked out a rusty but genuine laugh. Like, totally out loud. Flutters erupted in her stomach. Desperate to kiss him, she stepped closer. He must have sensed her intent, because he glanced over his shoulder, his eyes already blazing.

A hard knock sounded at the door.

Conrad groaned. "Beau, come to fetch you from my clutches?"

"Yep. But how'd you know it was him?"

He shook his head, a rueful smile playing at the corner of his lips. "I'd recognize that moment ruiner's knock anywhere."

With a laugh, Jane kissed his cheek, then rushed to the door, welcoming the hunky war vet inside. "Welcome to our —I mean, Conrad's, only Conrad's—home." The blush returned with a vengeance. "My stay is temporary."

Beau rolled his eyes. "You might as well tattoo his name on your bicep and buy yourself a pair of mom jeans, Janie."

Ignore the longing consuming your entire being. "I'll have you know I'm five seconds away from calling Sora and inviting her to stay in town for a while."

That wiped the smile off his face in a hurry.

Jane smirked, then sashayed off. He followed her to the kitchen. "Do not call Sora, Jane. I mean it."

"Are you saying I should text her instead?"

"Do not text her, Jane. Do not contact her in any way, shape or form."

She pretended to be aghast. "And cage my inner match-maker? How can you so cruelly suggest such a thing?"

Beau once spent weeks with the lovely Sora, guarding her

from dangerous criminals. The pair had snipped and snapped at each other constantly, but dang if their chemistry hadn't singed Jane's lashes. A hot-off-the-charts secret clearly brewed between the pair. But what? Jane would love a chance to solve that particular mystery.

The men nodded a bros-rule greeting at each other.

"Don't skimp on the butter," Beau said, plopping down on the window seat, leaving two barstools for her and Conrad.

"Who says you get any?" Conrad asked, even as he prepared a third plate.

Beau smirked at him, mimicking Jane. "What's with the framed campaign poster?"

This was payback for threatening his precious butter, no doubt about it.

Conrad loaded his arms with the plates, his skill something any waiter would envy. "Jane did a great job on the design. I especially like…"

Her breath caught. Even Beau went still, seeming to wait for Conrad to go for gold or chicken out. The moment of truth.

"…the font," he finally said, and her shoulders slumped with relief. Not disappointment? No, no. Only relief.

They settled in and Jane smoothed a napkin in her lap. "By the way. We should have a campaign meeting to discuss everything that's happened and how we're going to spin it. Someone must oversee the health of your reputation, Conrad, and that someone is me."

"Dr. Jane." Conrad smiled. "You wear many hats, sweetheart. In more ways than one."

Beau nodded with enthusiasm. "So many."

As she preened at them, the boys dove into their meal. "Did you learn anything about the mobster?" she asked her friend, not ready to experience her first taste yet.

"Not really." The vet finished off his French toast, paused

and grunted with satisfaction. "That was actually good. I'll have another."

Conrad rolled his eyes before passing the plate. "That was magnificent, and you know it."

Beau dug into a second with gusto, saying, "The only online chatter I've found comes from a *Headliner* thread. About two months ago, a group of people began speculating about the Gentleman's identity. We'll keep digging and find out who they are."

"Where and how did they hear about the Gentleman to begin with?"

"Don't know." He ate more.

Finally she gathered the courage and took a tentative bite of her boyfriend's supposed signature dish. Her eyes also widened. *You've got to be kidding me.* Sweet goodness! The decadence!

"Where are you two headed today?" Conrad's question penetrated her mind but she was too wrapped up in the flavor of perfection.

Jane shoveled in another bite, just to be sure she was tasting what she thought she was tasting. Then she took yet another bite. And another. This was, without a doubt, the most incredible masterpiece to ever grace her mouth.

"I'll let Jane tell you." Beau tilted his head as he watched her consume her next bite. "After she stops inhaling her food."

"What did you put in these, Conrad?" she demanded, licking pure maple syrup from her finger. "Some type of magic elixir?" As his baby blues twinkled delight at her, she remembered his question. "We're going to speak with Ashley Katz at the *Headliner.*"

The world's best chef told her, "I wish you all the best. Barrow questioned her last night but didn't learn much. She refused to share her sources without a warrant, which he hopes to have by the end of the day. Even then, I suspect she'll balk."

Jane smiled sweetly at him. "No problem. I don't need a warrant to get answers."

CHAPTER FIVE

Thou shall never let your boyfriend forget to wave to the
crowds and flex those biceps.

–Jane Ladling's Campaign Companion Code

*J*ane and Beau drove through downtown
Aurelian Hills, one of her favorite areas. Her
phone beeped, signaling a text. She meant to
check the message but got lost in the historical buildings
interwoven with modern architecture instead. Old-fashioned light posts lined the streets and the storefront displays
advertised winter sales.

Only when her phone buzzed a second time did she snap
out of her cozy haze. Jane dug inside her purse. When her
gaze snagged on the screen, she groaned.

> Tiffinator: So I walked the grounds or whatever. Things look as creepy as always, FYI. When are you coming back? I'm STARVING and without transportation. Oh! I'm happy to watch Rolex. He's my favorite thing about you.

She heaved a sigh. Because the beast staying in her home spoke so highly of the world's most perfect feline, Jane would do the unthinkable and loan her the hearse.

> Jane: I rode with Beau, so you can drive my car to pick up food. Keys are in my office with a tag that reads LAST RIDE TAXI SERVICE.

A minute passed without a new message.

> Tiffinator: 1) I found the key. 2) There's no way I'm driving that death carriage. 3) I'm guessing the key with the GRADE A MAN MEAT tag is Conrad's?

> Jane: I won't confirm or deny #3. If you want to be a baby and not drive a perfectly safe and comfortable vehicle, there's a tater tot casserole in the fridge. Cook it for an hour at 350.

> Tiffinator: Like, in an oven?

Oh, sweet goodness.

> Jane: Never mind. Order pizza. Just know they refuse to deliver straight to the door. They'll leave the pie on the benches at the Reflection Center. You can pay online with YOUR credit card.

Jane stored the phone in her handbag and pursed her lips at Beau as he eased into an open parking space at their destination. "I blame you."

"For what?" he sputtered.

"You know what! Ms. Tiffany Hotchkins!"

He rolled his eyes. "Though I refuse to admit I've done anything wrong, I'm happy to help you forget her." A calculating gleam lit his beautiful green irises. "Valentine's Day is coming up, and you haven't bought Conrad a present."

Eek! "You monster!" This was her first Valentine's Day with Conrad. How could she have overlooked such an important holiday? Though, yes, even when she'd dated Christopher Wellington, a firefighter who'd dumped her without warning, she had tended to avoid anything romantic.

"See? You're not thinking about Tiffany." Beau said with a smirk. "You're welcome."

Oh! "What are you getting Sora?" she asked, batting her lashes at him. "Do you need help composing a love sonnet?"

The smirk vanished. "Conrad is right. You really are a brat," he muttered.

"A label I cherish."

He slid out of the truck and jogged over to help her out. Wind blew as they motored forward. Jane adjusted the lapels of her coat, then fiddled with the ridiculous beret she now resented.

Well, onward and upward. Chin up, she entered the lobby of Aurelian Hills Media. The building housed three top of the line businesses. The AM station, the community's new Maker Space, and the *Headliner*.

Beau strode in behind her, handsome in a Peach State Security polo, khakis and rugged work boots. Like before, the lobby bustled with people and activity. Only now, a combo metal detector and security gate blocked the hallway leading to the various offices. A newly hired guard checked IDs.

Great! There'd be no marching straight to Ms. Katz's office, as Jane had done last time. With a sigh, she tugged Beau to the building's directory, pretending to study it.

"This won't be as easy as I thought," she admitted at low volume. They needed a distraction. "Quick, flex your arm. Do it!"

He immediately complied.

"No wait. This moment calls for unbuttoning."

Without missing a beat, Beau unfastened his wrist cuffs and rolled up the sleeves. Muscles engaged, adding both definition and bulge to his arms.

"Very nice," Jane told him, nodding her approval.

"So why am I doing this?" he asked.

She pressed her lips together to keep from smiling. "You'll see."

Turning on her heel, she led him toward the reception desk. A pretty brunette perched behind it, gaping at him. Excellent. The woman would be so besotted, she'd agreed to anything Beau asked. His good looks were such a great tool in her investigative arsenal. She might not have a fancy badge or access to high-tech equipment, but she had a sizzling hot friend, and that was far better.

At the halfway point, Jane nudged Beau with her shoulder. "Pretend you know how to flirt and charm her. Score us an immediate appointment with Ashley Katz. I believe in you," she added.

The war vet gave her a *girl please* look. "You baking me another casserole if—when—I succeed?"

"Beauregard," she said, batting her lashes at him. "I'll whip up an entire feast."

"Then you can consider this done." In an instant, his every feature grew serious. His body hummed with purpose.

She almost felt sorry for the receptionist. The poor woman wouldn't know what hit her. He was a mind-scrambler.

Oh no. Memories of his disastrous attempt at speed dating popped into Jane's mind. Something they'd done while investigating the death of journalist Ana Irons. Jane's smile slowly faded. The man may be hot enough to fry your brain, but he had zero skills in the romance department.

No matter. She would run interference if he veered off track.

"May I help you?" the brunette asked, fanning her cheeks.

Beau smiled sweetly. "Ms. Ladling and Mr. Harden to see Ms. Katz. We have a 9:30 appointment."

Jane opened her mouth to help him, only to go quiet and jerk her gaze to his face. An appointment? This wasn't a ruse?

His smile widened. "Ashley called me to ask about the crime scene," he explained, "and I snagged her first available slot."

She snorted. Just for that… "His name is Beau. He's single and ready to mingle," she told the receptionist. "What's your name, and are *you* single?"

"Oh. Um. Bonnie. Bonnie Happly. Y-yes. I am."

Beau offered Ms. Happly a soft smile. "I apologize for my friend. She's nosy."

This is for your own good, bud. "He doesn't know it, but he's ready to settle down with the right woman. Though be fore-warned. He might be hung up on a very special lady who—"

"I'm not hung up on anyone," he insisted with a nervous laugh.

Liar! He missed Sora, guaranteed. Maybe Jane should call her. Or invite her to the upcoming feast.

Hold up. Had Beau expertly manipulated Jane into planning an event and returning the beautiful heiress into his orbit, allowing him to see the object of his affections while maintaining his innocence?

Well played, Harden. Very well played.

"That's, um, wonderful for you." The receptionist nibbled on her bottom lip. "I'll let Ms. Katz know you've arrived. Please go on back." With a shy smile aimed at Beau, she handed each of them a visitor's badge, then waved to the security guard at the gate.

"You're the one who's welcome," Jane muttered to Beau as they walked away. "Conrad and I are happy to double with you and Grace. But when you fall in love and get married, I expect your firstborn to bear my name."

"Yep. A brat," Beau said without heat, giving his head an exasperated shake.

She fluffed her hair. "Thank you. I try."

The guard checked their IDs and allowed them to go through the metal detector. They continued down the hallway until reaching Ms. Katz's door. Jane took a second to focus before mimicking Conrad and rapping the entrance twice. One must be at her best when dealing with a second nemesis.

"Enter," Ashley called, and dang it, she sounded prepared. Overly eager even.

Deep breath in, out. *I can do this.* Jane marched inside, determined to get answers.

Beau followed her in and sealed them within.

"Hello, Jane," Ashley said, queen of the world behind her desk. She'd secured her hair in a knot on the top of her head, with a few curls hanging free of the clip. In a tailored beige blazer over a burgundy top, she exuded elegance and polish. The only exception was the tension marring her bold features.

"Hello." Not much had changed since Jane visited last November. The white board had been moved closer to the bank of monitors displaying the current goings on with various *Headliner* message boards.

The reporter linked her fingers and rested her joined hands atop the desk. Tone formal, she said, "Thank you for coming."

"Thank you for agreeing to see us." Jane and Beau settled in the chairs before the desk. She withdrew her notepad, Truth Be Told, and the printed article Ms. Katz had written about the deputy, with dozens of Jane's notes scribbled in the margins.

LED lights flickered on a compact recording device near the phone, catching her attention. Jane blurted out, "This conversation is off the record!"

"Yes, yes, fine. Why don't we just dive in?" Ashley nodded, as if answering her own question. She twisted in her seat, pointing to the names on the whiteboard. "From what I've been able to piece together, Joshua Gunn suspected six people of wanting him dead. You and I made the cut. I can guess the reason he ascribed to us. Destroying Conrad's competition and my story."

Very good. The reporter nailed it. Why so stressed, though? Was she, perhaps, consumed by guilt and trying to hide it? Afraid she was soon to be caught? "Is that why did you agreed to meet with me? To score a quote about finding the body?"

"Forget the body. Look, I know your hotshot husband isn't my biggest fan but—"

"Boyfriend!" Jane bellowed, almost rocketing from her seat. "He's my boyfriend. We aren't even engaged yet. Not that we'll ever get engaged. I refuse to wed. There's a family curse, you see, and I—"

Beau coughed, silencing her. "Concentrate, Janie," he whispered.

Right. Cheeks burning, she waved a hand in Ashley's direction. "You were saying?"

"Let's just forget Agent—Mr. Ryan for the moment. I'm going to ask you a question, Jane, and I need you to be honest with me." The reporter gripped the edge of her desk and leaned forward. "Did Deputy Gunn receive threatening letters?"

Hmm. To answer or not to answer. She would never betray Conrad's confidence, or put his new consultant gig in jeopardy. Was this something GBH wanted kept quiet? "Why do you suspect this?"

Ashley's gaze darted to Beau. Did she hope he'd offer a better response?

He crossed his arms, tilted his head, and remained silent. A Beau Harden special.

"Let's try this another way," Ashley said. "What do you know about the Gentleman?"

"Only that no one claims to have seen him or spoken to him, yet he's gained a terrible reputation," Jane replied honestly. "What do *you* know?"

Repeatedly thumping an ink pen against the edge of the desk, the reporter finally relented, "Three months ago, Mr. Gunn came to me. Told me he feared for his life, and if I didn't run a piece about a mobster called the Gentleman, warning the citizens of Aurelian Hills of the snake in their midst, he would arrest me for something. Anything. I didn't take kindly to his threat, so I ran the article—focused on Gunn. And what I wrote was a hundred percent accurate because I am my own source. And while a journalist never wishes to become the story, I was hoping to preempt Mr. Gunn's lies, if ever he followed through."

Jane listened, reeling. Wow, wow, wow. Talk about a boatload of information to digest. Deputy Gunn had been desperate, willing to break the law and ruin someone's future to spread the crime boss news. Apparently the deputy had suspected the Gentleman's identity. A snake the residents trusted. Unless Ashley lied?

Gut check. Jane...ugh! Was she on the right track or not? Why, why, why had her gut gone silent? "Did the deputy contact you after your investigation hit the presses?" Would Ashley admit Gunn planned to "sue for millions?"

"He did." The reporter seemed to brace herself for a blow. "He called and accused me of being on the Gentleman's payroll. Told me I'd endangered innocent lives. That, when everyone found out how I'd attempted to discredit the only person willing to take on such a hardened criminal, I alone was to blame for their deaths. Now, I think the individual who killed Gunn is after me."

Ashen, she poked at her cell phone and passed the device to Jane, her grip trembly. A photo of a letter filled the screen. That letter resembled those the deputy received.

"It arrived this morning," Ashley said. "Found it in my inbox, delivered here at the station."

The magazine cut-outs read, *Forget the Gentleman or DIE*

"Is GBH aware?" Jane ached for anyone in the crosshairs of a killer. While she and the other woman had often been at odds, she empathized with her greatly. Once she'd been a target herself. On the other hand, she wasn't sure she could trust the reporter. What if Deputy Gunn had been right and Ashley killed him to keep him from discrediting her, then mailed herself a letter to use as proof of her innocence? It was possible. Every other murderer Jane had caught had blamed someone else. Why not this one?

Lawsuit aside, there was still motive. If Deputy Gunn had become sheriff—not that he'd had a chance of beating

Conrad at the ballot box—he could have made the journalist's life a nightmare. If Ashley was innocent and wasn't on
the Gentleman's payroll, however, she was in grave danger.

"Before you guys showed up, I called Special Agent
Barrow and Mr. Ryan. We have an appointment in an hour."

"Good." Until Jane's gut recovered from whatever
ailment currently plagued it, she'd give the crack reporter
the benefit of the doubt. Because…just because. "You might
not trust the authorities, but I assure you Conrad Ryan will
never jeopardize your life. He's honest, dependable, and
trustworthy, and he'll help keep you safe while we hunt this
scoundrel."

"Give me the okay, and I'll put a security detail on you,"
Beau piped up. "He'll trail you when you leave this building
and ensure you arrive home safely. He'll even check your
house and fortify any weaknesses."

"I—yes," the other woman replied in a relieved rush,
nodding. "That's a good idea. I was planning to sleep in my
office since there's a guard downstairs, so thank you. I'm not
letting go of this story and plan to launch my own investigation. By the time I'm done, the Gentleman won't be harming
anyone ever again."

Hey! That was Jane's line. But no matter. Rather than
boast about her success rate, she would simply solve the
crime first. There was a chance the Gentleman might turn
his murderous sights on the lawmen hot on his trail. Better
nip him in the bud fast.

"Do you have any clues about the Gentleman's identity?"
she asked.

"Not yet, but I'll start with those who've mentioned the
mobster on the *Headliner*."

Excellent. But Jane wasn't inclined to rest solely on the
reporter's intel. She intended to ask Beau to speed up his
digging. Maybe invite the boys to help. She also aimed to

ramp up her questions for Thomas Bennett when she visited the Gold Star Lounge tonight.

"Thank you for your time." She stashed the printed article and notepad in her purse. While this meeting hadn't gone as she'd expected, she'd learned something, adding fuel to the fires of her determination. "I truly appreciate it."

"Honestly, I planned to pump you for information while revealing nothing before I saw the letter," Ashley said as they both stood.

"Then we had the same strategy," she admitted ruefully.

For the first time in their acquaintance, they shared a small but genuine smile.

Maybe the all-caps texting reporter was guilty of Gunn's murder, maybe not. If Jane had to render a verdict right this second, though, she'd say innocent, but she wouldn't be satisfied. She'd have a better idea of the case as a whole after she spoke with Mr. Bennett.

"Before I go," Jane said, "I wanted to ask if you'd interview Conrad for his campaign."

"Certainly," the reporter replied, a familiar gleam appearing in her dark eyes. "I'll expect an exclusive, of course."

"Deal. You'll get twenty-four-hours. I can only hold back the other outlets for so long. I'll have Conrad call you to set up a time."

Jane and Beau exited the office and made their way out of the building.

"Yes, I'll dig deeper and faster into the *Headliner*," he said. "I'll even get Trick's help."

He knew her so well. "Perfect."

The moment they were inside his truck, her seatbelt secured, Beau firmly stated, "I don't think you should work this case, Jane. It's more dangerous than I realized. This new threat..."

Whoa. That was so not what she'd expected to hear. This was the first time the vet had ever pulled a Conrad and suggested she not do something. Always before, he'd been eager to help. "Let a possible crime boss win my town? Never. In fact, I'm going to double my efforts. I'm not sorry to tell you this, Beauregard, but nothing can stop me now."

CHAPTER SIX

Thou shall never let your boyfriend forget he serves you first and the people second.

–Jane Ladling's Campaign Companion Code

*P*reparation was the key to success. Jane crammed her purse with everything she thought she might need for an evening of investigating at the Gold Star Lounge. The notecards she'd peppered with hard-hitting questions for Mr. Bennett. Truth Be Told. Lip gloss. ID, cell phone, and a credit card.

Money-wise, she wouldn't let herself spend more than twenty dollars. The cemetery's trust left little money for anything but survival. Sometime she supplemented her family income with midnight tours and game night parties, but business had slowed since the last dead body was found on the premises.

Oh! A weapon! She should take a weapon. Considering she might come face to face with Deputy Gunn's murderer, and said murderer might have an army of henchmen at his disposal, she should be prepared to defend Conrad's very life.

But what could she use? Jane scanned her small, somewhat cluttered bedroom. Her gaze slipped over curtains held open by the ever-present cat hammock, the patchwork quilt in shades of lilac, purple and lavender that adorned her bed and the hats stacked next to the antique nightstand. Hats. Hat pins. Of course. She shoved several in the purse's side pocket.

Rolex and Tiffany watched from her bed. The black cat was curled up on the widow's lap, purring with such force he nearly shook the entire cottage. Jane was overjoyed he'd found love again; his last crush, Cartier, had been taken from him unexpectedly—long story. But did he have to enjoy the attention of his mother's nemesis so much?

"You're wearing the wrong dress for the Gold Star Lounge," Tiffany announced. "You need something that screams money and whispers secret dreams. Preferably tight and black. Zero frills."

"This dress is perfect for any location." Jane smoothed her hands down the cotton A-line. She'd purposely avoided her preferred fit and flare style. Which was totally different from an A-line, thank you.

"It's too cutesy. I mean, really, Jane. You're wearing smiling hamburgers."

"Yes, and they are adorable," she stated, adjusting her pillbox hat with netting the color of ketchup. She treasured this dress. Grandma Lily made it for her. In fact, Jane had an entire section of her closet devoted to the "happy" collection her amazing grandmother had sewed. Smiling pancakes and kittens and hats.

Tiffany gave her a pointed look, as if no other words needed to be spoken. "Why are you visiting the lounge, anyway? The drinks are overpriced, and the food is snobby."

"Food can be snobby?" Wait. The beautiful brunette might

know some of the workers personally. A valid reason to do what she'd previously refused to do and name a name. "Do you know Thomas Bennett, a bartender?"

"Thomas..." Tiffany's eyes widened. "You mean Tom Cat? The guy who eavesdrops on private conversations because he's constantly on the prowl for a sugar momma, the older and richer the better?"

"Maybe?" And hmmm. If Mr. Bennett was indeed this "Tom Cat," he'd had plenty of motive to kill Gunn. Being forced to become the deputy's CI had probably screwed with his prowling and endangered his life.

Tiffany shuddered. "He's a creep to the bone. You're in for a miserable night."

Miserable while solving a murder with Conrad at her side to watch her do it? Hardly!

A hard double rap sounded at the front door. Jane jolted, her heart leaping. Conrad!

Grinning, she rushed over to give Rolex a scratch behind the ears. "Momma loves you, baby. Never forget that." Her gaze shot to the widow. "Call me immediately if there's a problem. And don't forget he eats dinner at eight. And ten. And sometimes 10:57 on the dot for reasons he'll explain when he's ready. Remember, he likes fresh water before, during and after each feeding. Oh! And the volume on the TV should be between twelve and fourteen, never lower and never higher. If he stands at the front door and meows, he wants you to go outside so he can have the house to himself. It's his private time, and he works hard for it."

"He's an extra special good boy, I get it," Tiff replied, her tone dry as sand. "He'll be fine, promise."

"He deserves better than fine." Jane blew the precious kisses as she backed out of the room.

Once the feline and his crush were out of sight, she drew in a deep breath. *Let's do this.*

Down the stairs she went. Conrad waited in her living room. To her surprise, Beau and Isaac were with him. Before allowing herself to gobble up the future sheriff with her gaze, she greeted her friends with hugs.

Beau looked gorgeous in a pair of well-tailored blue pants and a crisp white shirt that accentuated his broad shoulders and muscled arms. Isaac also stunned in sleek, charcoal gray slacks and a light blue dress shirt, his impeccable style on full display.

As for Conrad... Their gazes met, and for a moment, the rest of the world disappeared. The man stole her breathe. A tailored ivory shirt and black trousers graced his solid frame. From his dark hair to his polished shoes, he radiated confidence.

He slid his baby blues over her, a smile curving one corner of his mouth. "You are a gift."

She preened, loving the way he looked at her. Anyway. No need to bring love into it. Moving on. Rising on her tiptoes, she kissed his stubbled cheek. He wound an arm around her waist, surrounding her with his warmth and scent. Goosebumps broke out over her limbs.

"Will you be as foolish as our dear friend Beau and ask me to stay home where it's safe from possible crime bosses and their employees?" she asked, sifting strands of his silken hair between her fingers.

"I will not," Conrad replied. "I'm a good boy today. I even set up a campaign interview with Ashley Katz, as you so sweetly demanded I do. It's happening in two weeks."

"You guys suck," Beau said with a bona fide man-pout. "Every other case, you told me I needed to learn how to tell Jane no."

"And I stand by that." Conrad grinned at her. "I learned to tell her yes."

Oh, how she adored the men in her life.

Jane practically floated to Conrad's SUV. She rode up front with him, regulating the military buddies to the back. The twenty-minute drive passed too quickly, but she used the time to dole out notecards to each of her companions.

"These are the questions you will ask Mr. Bennett," she explained. "As you guys badger him for information, I'll sneak in and extract tidbits of truth from his brain."

Beau read aloud. "What's the funniest thing you've ever witnessed a cat do? What kind of music feeds your soul?" His gaze flipped up, landing on her. "What, no asking about his favorite color?"

"Someone didn't read the back of his card, I see," she said, a patient teacher with a struggling student. "Obviously, these questions are designed to help us establish his true character. Do your best to introduce each subject organically."

"This is my real punishment, isn't it?" Beau deadpanned.

In lieu of an answer, she blew him a kiss.

Outside her window, twinkle lights flickered in the dormant trees that lining Main Street. An amber glow from streetlamps illuminated a busy sidewalk. People bustled on foot, to various shops and eateries their breath visible in the chilly air.

Nestled in the heart of downtown Aurelian Hills, the Gold Star Lounge dazzled. It didn't open until seven in the evening and then only on Tuesday, Friday and Saturday. No one knew why. Just as no one knew who owned the place. The website listed it as an LLC, promising refined entertainment and unforgettable memories.

They parked in the lot between a Porsche and a Jaguar and made their way to the door. With three muscular males surrounding her, she kinda felt like a movie star. The crisp air carried hints of burning wood and smoky cologne. Laughter and music teased her ears.

The aged brownstone set between two other brownstones, with stairs leading to the basement of Aurelian Hills's original general store. A place rumored to be a speakeasy during prohibition years. Excitement raced through Jane as they descended the steps and entered another world...

Velvet drapes in rich emerald cascaded from the ceiling, framing different spaces in luxury. Everything from the framed artwork, mirrors and decorative molding were gilded in gold. Several opulent chandeliers bathed the space in gentle light, while plush chair cushions whispered an invitation to indulge.

Smooth jazz seduced in the background. More patrons filled the club than Jane had anticipated. A handful of couples slow danced on a parquet floor. Other people stood or sat in groups, sipping cocktails and conversing. A plethora of different notes and tones created a cornucopia of sound.

At the center of it all, Mayor Thacker held court. He exuded charm and a keen awareness of his own power. His silver-streaked hair added a touch of maturity to his captivating, if forced, personality. Beside him stood his wife, stiffly outfitted in a meticulously crafted burgundy silk dress. Jane began to understand Tiffany's warning.

The First Lady of Aurelian Hills clearly disapproved of whatever the woman across from her was saying; her lips curved in a sneer. Now come on! Jane was a baby when it came to aiding a boyfriend running for office, but she knew better than to broadcast disapproval at constituents.

Beau gave her shoulder a nudge before he and Isaac split from their group. Anyone with a pulse glanced at the ex-soldiers at least once. A few onlookers outright stared at the double-your-trouble yum-yums while whispering and giggling behind their hands.

Placing a strong hand on her lower back, Conrad led her to a table near the bar. He nodded at the occupants, who

GENA SHOWALTER & JILL MONROE

nodded in return, stood and walked off, gifting the table to them.

She sputtered as she sat. "But why...how."

"Beau isn't the only one who can plan ahead." Conrad grinned as he claimed the chair beside her. "Bennett is behind the bar."

Her gaze zoomed to the area in question, and she almost squealed with excitement. She had the perfect view of a tall, dark and handsome young man mixing drinks, wearing a name tag that read Tom.

Ding, ding, ding. The suspect. "Don't be mad if I completely ignore you," she said, keeping her attention on her target.

Conrad chuckled. "This isn't my first rodeo, sweetheart."

Jane tried to reply, she really did, but too many thoughts crowded her mind. *A creep, Tiff?* Tom Cat smiled at anyone who ordered, cracked jokes with certain patrons and politely rebuffed any under thirty who hit on him, and flirted with the older gals, making them feel special, as evidenced by their tips. Was that an act? Did he play favorites to score one of those sugar mamas the widow mentioned? A long con sort of thing?

Or maybe Tiffany had misjudged him. Maybe he'd changed since the two last occupied the same space?

No, Tiff was right. His actions triggered Jane's sixth sense—suspicion. Because yeah, everything he did, from the expressions he donned to the way he poured drinks, seemed practiced. But the most telling part? He didn't bear a single pet hair on his clothing.

Conrad leaned over and kissed the racing pulse at the base of her neck. His warm breath tickled her skin, inciting a new round of goose bumps. "What do you think of him so far?"

The first word to pop into her head once she finished shivering? "Smooth."

"Agreed." He eased back in his chair. "I don't know about you, but I'm ready to take this stake out to the next level and get face to face with him. Today we learned the drug used was fentanyl. It wasn't in his coffee grounds or pot, only in the mug he drank from. Someone had to be in the house to add it."

"And since the deputy disabled his security system, it stands to reason he knew and trusted his killer."

"Or the killer deactivated the alarm and sneaked in."

Good pointed. Did Mr. Bennett possess that level of skill? With his alleged connection to the Gentleman, he wouldn't have any trouble scoring drugs. "Don't worry. I'll get us some answers." She pressed a swift kiss into Conrad's lips, silencing any reply.

But reply he did, just not the way she expected. Catching her by the nap, he held her in place. "Are you going to stay with me again tonight?" The words whispered against her heated skin.

"I...am." No need to think. He'd learned to tell her yes, he'd said; well, she'd learned to trust him with her future. Kind of. Mostly.

He brushed a lock of hair behind her ear, and her heart fluttered. Before she did something to make a fool of herself, she stood. "I'm ready to subtly question him."

"Eager to get this done so you can have me all to yourself? I understand." Conrad winked and rose, then motioned her forward.

Her heart did more of that fluttering as they sidled up to the bar.

Bennett noticed them and smiled his patented smile. "What can I get you?"

"Did you kill Deputy Josh Gunn?" she asked, getting

straight to the heart of the matter. Yes, and there went her carefully planned questions.

Thomas went real pale real fast. "Who are you?"

"Jane Ladling, with special consultant to the GHB, Conrad Ryan. Don't run," she added. "Our men have got you surrounded."

Conrad made the slightest shift from side to side, and for some reason, Bennett grew paler.

"Not this again." The bartender sighed and motioned to a door before wiping his hands on a towel. "Let's go in back." He told a coworker, "I'm taking my smoke break."

The women behind Jane groaned with disappointment.

"You don't smoke and we're slammed," the coworker cried, but with a look from him she changed her tune. "Sure, sure. Go on. That's fine," she called next. "Take as long as you need."

As Jane and Conrad followed him past the door, her boyfriend rasped, "You couldn't break it to him easy?"

"It was loud and crowded in there. I saved time and energy, two of my favorite things." They strode down a narrow hallway and into a cramped break room.

Kegs and boxes filled with whisky, gin and bourbon were crammed into the tight space. A small table with two mismatched chairs had been shoved into the corner for employees to grab a quick snack. The air smelled of pine cleaner, deli meat, and stale beer.

Bennett spun, his jovial mask stripped away, revealing anger. "First the cops came, then some reporter, now you. But I didn't kill Deputy Gunn. I wouldn't."

"Let's talk about your arrest," Conrad said, stuffing his hands in his pockets. "You served as his CI. What evidence did you gather for him?"

Oh, good question!

"How many times do I need to say it?" Bennett burst out.

"I've never been and will never be a confidential informant. Not even for Gunn. He was kind to me once, so I slipped him a free beer the few times he'd come in, but that's the extent of our relationship."

Now hold up a sec. "Going to deny knowledge of the Gentleman too?"

"Yes. I'll tell you what I told Gunn. I don't know anyone who goes by that name." He made a scoffing sound. "I have no idea why the deputy suspected me of trying to kill him except, maybe, out of spite. I dated his daughter, and he hated that."

Connections kept snapping into place.

Bennett scrubbed a hand over his face. "The deputy planted those drugs and arrested me. The prosecutor saw the holes in the case and dropped the charges at my arraignment. But I knew Gunn wouldn't stop until I dumped Madeline, so I did. Our association ended there. So did the free booze."

Hmmm. Was this another performance? With Gunn out of the way, Bennett had a clean slate and an open road. No one to disprove his story. No one to force him to spy on a dangerous crime boss. No one to keep him away from a still loved girlfriend.

Who did Jane believe? The deputy who'd also accused *her* of being a possible murderer or the guy suspected of conning older women out of their money?

"Where were you Saturday morning?" Conrad asked.

"With someone. I stayed the night at her place."

"What's her name?" Conrad persisted, but Bennetts remained silent. "She's your alibi, so you can't keep the information secret if you hope to escape charges."

The bartender popped his jaw. "Jessica Thacker. But I don't think she'll willingly share details pertaining to our time together. I snuck in while the husband snored in bed."

Oh, ick. Wait. The *mayor's wife* had slept with Bennett?

The married woman who spent her days reading to children at the library and planting trees for the Aurelian Hills Beautification Project had fallen for Tom Cat's charm?

Jane planned on asking the woman directly. "I hope you *don't* know the Gentleman. He killed once, and threatened to do it again, starting with anyone connected to this case." At least, that was what the letter sent to Ashley Katz inferred, in Jane's humble opinion.

Any lingering color in Bennett's face drained, leaving him ghostly. "I don't know the Gentleman," he insisted. He shook his head for emphasis. "If you'll excuse me, break time is over."

He stomped off.

"Vote Conrad Ryan for sheriff!" Jane called, but he was already gone.

"Somewhere in that mess is the truth," Conrad muttered. "But he's definitely afraid of something. Or someone."

"Yes. And that someone seems to be the Gentleman he knows nothing about." She thought for a moment. "I bet Gunn's estranged daughter, Madeline, could help us shed some light on the situation."

"Possibly."

As they re-entered the lounge, Jane's gaze shot to the Thacker's table. Well, well, well. The couple was gone.

CHAPTER SEVEN

Always be camera ready, even if your guy isn't in the picture.

–Jane Ladling's Campaign Companion Code

*L*ater that night–far later–Jane shifted her gaze to Conrad. A smile bloomed. He'd fallen asleep on the couch, his hair tousled, his expression boyish. Long lashes cast spiky shadows over his cheeks. The dark stubble on his jaw had thickened, and she yearned to graze her fingertips over the prickle.

When they stopped at the cottage earlier today, before returning to his bungalow, she'd picked up a few essentials. The quilt her grandmother sewed. A stack of her favorite hats. Her knitting supplies. Framed pictures of the people dearest to her. One with Fiona, Grandma Lily, and Jane's Pops, Gary, the other with Jane, Conrad and Rolex.

The quilt now draped Conrad, keeping him toasty warm while Jane sat cross-legged on the floor, a laptop balanced on the coffee table. Cheddar was curled up next to her, snoozing like his father.

Rolex, the little darling, had chosen to remain at the cottage with Tiffany. Jane swallowed a whisper. She'd called and called and called for him on her way out the door, but he'd merely stared at her from the widow's lap. A travesty she refused to consider until later. Much later. At the moment, she was scouring social media sites for Thomas "Tom Cat" Bennett, Madeline Gunn, the Gentleman, Ashley Katz, Robert and Jessica Thacker, and Denise Allen.

Tom enjoyed posting shirtless photos of himself with "inspirational" messages that had nothing to do with his pose, location or the state of his undress. Gems like: "Remember to breathe." "Leap because ambition gives you wings." "Fly even when physics disagrees." What he didn't post? Anything connected to drugs or the Gentleman. He didn't even include pictures of women. Nothing with the alleged sugar mommas or Madeline. But something Jane did find interesting were his posts featuring a countdown. Why did he do this?

As for Madeline herself, Jane learned she was a mortician who worked at Aurelian Hills Cemetery. The worst place on Earth! They drove golf carts over their plots and didn't take the opinions of their residents seriously.

Every day, Madeline shared intimate details of her life. Places she went, foods she ate, people she saw, doctors she visited. Guys she dated. But for some reason, there were no mentions of Tom. Why not advertise their relationship as she'd done with everyone else? No mention of her father's death, either. In fact, her updates since his passing seemed more upbeat than usual.

In many of the most recent over shares, she referred to a dude she'd once dated as "the Forbidden Fruit." A subtle reference to Tom, perhaps? Because he worked for a mobster? Because her father hated him? Or both?

According to Madeline, the Forbidden Fruit cheated

often, only cared for money and lied constantly. A description that very much jived with Tiffany's opinion of Tom Cat. A man like that wouldn't hesitate to kill the deputy for endangering his livelihood.

Oh, oh! In one thread, Madeline mentioned getting a cut and color from none other than Denise Allen. How interesting. The deputy's estranged daughter spent an hour with the deputy's (ex)girlfriend. What if the two discussed ways to off him? But what would be their motive?

When you need answers, start digging.

Using an app, Jane booked her own appointment with Denise for tomorrow at 12:15. Or today, she realized when she noticed the time. 2:47 in the morning. She should probably go to bed, but she wasn't even tired...a thought instantly belied by a jaw-cracking yawn. No matter. She pressed through, determined to learn something, anything, about the Gentleman.

Just in case Ashley had published any revealing articles on the man—or woman—Jane opened up the *Headliner*. But, though she searched, she found only the reporter's newest post. A message with only five words: *I Will Not Be Silent.*

Okay, maybe the woman was kind of a little bit amazing.

"You should be asleep, sweetheart." Conrad's raspy voice caressed her ears a split second before he settled his hands on her shoulders, rubbing sore muscles.

A moan parted her lips. Oh, that felt good. "Don't stop," she whispered, leaning into his touch.

He kissed the top of her head and sat behind her, continuing the massage. "Learned anything interesting?"

Her eyelids grew heavy as tension drained from her muscles. "The Gentleman is a thorn in my side," she muttered, giving Conrad's strong hands more of her weight. "Why is he known as the Gentleman, anyway? Does he say please and thank you while committing the most vile acts? Or is he the total opposite?"

"We'll figure it out. We won't stop until we succeed." A teasing note entered his voice. "That's the Ryan family motto."

She craned her neck to pen him with a lethal stare, but mmm, his palms were so warm. Forgetting what she'd planned to say, she melted deeper into his touch and sighed with satisfaction.

Conrad petted her hair. "Rest your magnificent brain. We need you at your most suspicious."

"Wrong. You just need me," she corrected groggily, already drifting off...

❦ ❦ ❦ ❦

JANE WOKE UP WITH A GASP. She jolted upright, disturbing Cheddar, who cuddled at her side.

She'd fallen asleep on the couch again, and Conrad was nowhere to be seen. Frowning, she fished for her phone, finding it on the coffee table next to her laptop and a note.

She swiped up the paper and read. *Jessica denied sleeping with Bennett. Barrow and I will speak with him at the station later today.*

Her frown deepened. How had he found the time to interview Jessica Thacker?

Jane glanced at the clock and startled. 10:53 a.m. She'd slept the morning away. And dang it, she had a hair appointment in roughly an hour. As a sense of urgency sparked, she shot Tiffany a text.

> Jane: Can you arrange a meeting with
> Jessica Thacker for me? Today??? Consider
> it your first week's rent. It'll have to be
> sometime after noon, though, because I'm
> supposed to be at the beauty parlor at 12:15.

Then she messaged Fiona.

> Jane: Make me the happiest girl in the world
> and tell me we're on for blueberry pancakes
> tonight!

She didn't wait for their replies but bolted to her feet and hurried to the bathroom, where she showered, brushed her teeth, styled her hair and donned a cozy knit dress with a slightly flared skirt. She paired it with brown boots and a hat in the shape of a bow. Though her stomach gurgled, there was no time for breakfast.

Except, as she gathered her purse and keys, she found a file wrapped breakfast burrito Conrad had left for her on the kitchen counter. What a dear, darling man. She should marry him and lock him down before—Jane stopped that thought in its tracks. Her heart stopped, too. Or it seemed to. She had *not* just considered marriage an option. Nope. Not her. Not ever.

This temporary move-in had been a mistake. An abbreviation from the norm. A one-off. Blip. She'd gotten too cozy, and it showed. She'd have to do something drastic. Later. Shaking, she checked her phone and discovered a reply from both Tiffany and Fiona.

> Tiffinator: I'll get you in to see the first lady of
> our town—but only if you take me to the hair
> appointment.

Uh, why did she have to go?

> Jane: Fine! I'll be there in 10 minutes.

> Fionality: You bring the good time and I'll supply the food!

> Jane: I love you so much!

Jane reached the Garden in ten minutes, as predicted. She noticed Beau's truck idling outside the front gate and sighed. He planned to trail her today, didn't he? When he didn't follow her to the cottage, but remained beyond the grounds, waiting, she parked and texted him.

> Jane: You can ride with us, silly. No need to hide.

> Beaudyguard: Wasn't trying. I can be invisible when necessary, but still nearby at all times. Have fun today.

Grateful for him, she went inside. The widow sat in the living room, petting Rolex, and Jane knew she had to face facts. Her cat had fallen in love again, and there was nothing she could do about it except be there for him when it ended.

After giving the goodest boy all the kisses, she returned to the family vehicle with Tiffany in tow. The other woman wore a blush pink catsuit and black, spiky stiletto heels. If she hoped to prove she'd gotten back her groove, that outfit did the trick.

"Don't you have a normal car?" Tiffany asked, cringing as she buckled in.

"Why did you demand to accompany me to get a trim just to complain now?" With the twist of a key, the car's engine purred to life.

"Are you kidding? I've been cooped up with the dead and

needed to see living people. Even though the living are the worst."

"Sometimes. Most times. But not always." Proof: Conrad, Fiona, Beau, the triple stack yum-yums Holden, Trick and Isaac. "So? What time am I meeting with Mrs. Thacker?"

"*We* are having drinks with Jessie at the Treasure Room. Two sharp. And fair warning. If you think I'm a snob, wait till you meet her. Trust me, you require backup."

Jessie? Jane buried a series of groans, keeping her protests to herself as she eased onto the main road. In the name of justice, she could do anything–even tag team a murder suspect with Tiffany Hotchkins. And yes, Jessica Thacker was a suspect. How many lines would the woman cross to protect her alleged lover from the cop screwing with his future? Not to mention the fear of outing her affair. The blackmail potential was off the charts.

"What do you know about, um, Jessie?" Jane asked, catching sight of Beau's truck in her rearview mirror. "Rumor has it, she and Thomas Bennett are linked."

Tiffany wrinkled her nose. "She would never get involved with someone like Tom Cat. She eschews any hint of scandal."

They reached the wrought iron double doors of the Gilded Scissor Salon a few minutes later. Beau parked a good distance away, then remained many steps behind as they approached the shop. Two oversized windows flanked the door, both adorned with gauzy golden curtains that allowed only the tiniest glimpse of the inner sanctum dedicated to outer beauty.

Jane and Tiffany made their way inside. On the walls hung a mishmash of vintage posters of past styles, pictures of modern cuts, and decorations handmade by the staff. The sound of hairdryers, running water and laughter filled the space, as everyone caught up on the latest town gossip. Hair-spray and freshly brewed coffee scented the air.

"Ugh. So much hair," Tiffany said with another cringe, motioning to the different colored and textured locks being swept into a pile.

Had the widow never been inside a beauty shop? What, had a stylist always come to her home?

Denise turned the corner, tying a black apron with golden piping around her waist. She secured her newly dyed fire engine red hair in a high ponytail that bounced with each step. Jane had never seen her without bold cat-eye eyeliner. She wore an even bolder lip stain—the same product she sold —and a checkered black and blue miniskirt with vibrant pink tights. Over forty but young at heart, she dictated her own fashion.

She spotted Jane, put her fists on her hips, and said, "Jane Ladling. The moment your name popped up on my appoint-ment log, I knew why."

"Oh?"

The older woman nodded. "You want to question me about Joshie. And that's fine. I didn't like him toward the end, but I didn't want him dead. I'll help you catch the killer any way I can as long as I'm also working on your hair."

A deal worth taking. "Feel free to trim an inch or two," she said, sinking into the hot seat. Yes, she'd worn the same hairstyle for years, but she liked it. She'd cut the bangs after a breakup with Christopher. Now, the thick fringe boosted her confidence.

"Layer, too," Tiffany commanded. "She's growing out the bangs."

What! "Don't listen to her. She's wrong."

Denise stepped back and examined Jane as if she were a bug under a microscope. "No, she's right. You need layers." That said, she got busy securing a poncho around Jane's neck and leading her to a sink to wash her hair. "When did you two become friends?"

"I wouldn't say we're friends," Tiffany answered, sitting nearby.

The bell over the door tinkled, and Beau entered. He winked at Jane, then claimed a chair in the small waiting area. "Be with you in a moment, hon," Denise called, then lowered her voice. "Whew, that man is pure fire."

"I'd do him," eagerly called another stylist, who'd only scrolled on her phone up to this point. "His hair, I mean."

"You just sit your tush back in that seat, McKayla, and play your penguin bowling game," Denise chided. "I'm not losing out on my chance to suds a stud like that."

Jane choked, then cleared her throat. Well, only days ago she'd thought of Beau as a great weapon in her arsenal. Here he was, proving it. But okay, enough letting his presence distract her. Focus up. "While you were dating Deputy Gunn —Joshie—did he ever mention Tom Bennett or a crime boss known as the Gentleman?" Through Conrad, I knew she had. But would she lie?

"Yes and yes," Denise replied with an emphatic nod as she adjusted the temperature of the water. Color me impressed. She'd offered the truth. "Tom and this gentleman guy were all he discussed. It was a true obsession. I had no choice but to kick him to the curb. Do you know how frustrating it is dealing with nonstop blabbering over secret plots, hidden agendas, and crime networks? His paranoia was over the top."

Hmm. Usually people found *one* nice thing to spout about a deceased partner. Even a former partner. But Denise could only scrounge up a desire not to see the deputy die?

Conrad did like to say a significant other was most often responsible for a murder. Or he'd mentioned it once. What-ever. It had certainly turned out to be true when Jane's lawyer wound up murdered on her property, killed by his ex. And look at Ana Irons, offed by someone she'd dated for a story.

So, what would be Denise's motive for killing Gunn? Had he caught her doing something she shouldn't and threatened to expose her? Maybe he was the one who'd broken up with her, and she'd exacted revenge.

Warm water soaked Jane's hair. As the hairdresser's long, blunt-tipped nails massaged shampoo into the drenched mane, a floral fragrance filled her nostrils, and her eyelids fluttered closed. Mmm, this was heavenly. Maybe Denise was innocent.

"Did the deputy mention his feelings for Tom?" Jane asked, barely stopping herself from slurring the words.

"Oh yeah. Plenty. Joshie hated Tom with every fiber of his being," she said, rinsing out the shampoo and replacing it with coconut-scented conditioner. "Called the guy a jackal and swore to prove it to the whole town, especially his daughter."

Well, well. Hello motive. For the deputy and Tom *and* Madeline Gunn. "Did the deputy hate Tom enough to plant evidence and arrest him?"

"That, I'm not sure of." Denise wrung out her wet hair, wrapped the locks in a towel, and led her to a spinning chair. "He had a moral compass, but he didn't always consult it, if you know what I mean."

In other words, maybe he did, maybe he didn't. Jane tried a different route. "What crimes did he claim this Gentleman committed?" Racketeering? Extortion? Loan sharking? Tax evasion? Something connected to Tom? "And did he ever describe the Gentleman's appearance?"

Denise's expression scrunched up as she combed out Jane's wet hair. "To my recollection, he never mentioned specific details." She pinned locks up and tugged hunks straight. Then the cutting began. "Joshie—guess I should call him Josh now, huh. Anyway, he always spoke in generalities. Major up-and-coming bad guy. Breaks the law. Illegal activities. Blah, blah, blah. But I do think I have a file he worked on at the house. I'll send it your way if I find it."

"Yes, yes, yes!" Jane cut off a squeal of delight. When a long, dark lock fell to the floor, however, she gaped. Um, was she going to leave bald? "Is there anything else you're willing to share?"

"Maybe," Denise said after a moment of thought. "After I spoke with the inspector detective guys, I remembered Josh did tell me Tom was higher up in the cartel than he'd originally believed."

Ohhh. A detail Conrad needed to know. But was sharing case elements as if they were candy something Gunn did often? "Did the deputy discuss any other cases with you?"

"Nope. But then, he wasn't obsessed with anything else." Finally, Denise sheathed the scissors and grabbed the hair dryer. When she spun the chair, Jane lost her view of the mirror. Beau was no longer in sight.

Had he left, or was he trying to hide now?

As the other woman applied the finishing touches on her new style, Jane texted Conrad her hot tip.

> Jane: Tom Bennett might be higher up the Gentleman's food chain than we thought!

"Ta da! All done," Denise said, dramatically whisking off the poncho and spinning the chair for the big reveal.

When Jane caught a glimpse of her reflection, she forgot about her phone. Oh. Oh wow. Okay. This was kind of, well, amazingly awesome. She brushed her fingers through the silken locks. The layered pieces brought a delicacy to her features she'd never noticed before.

"Jane owes us both a huge tip," Tiffany said with all kinds of satisfaction.

"And yet Denise is the only one who's getting a dime," Jane replied. "You also get smiles and hugs. I'm rich in those." She popped up to hug the stylist, who merely patted her back. "Oh! Don't forget to vote Conrad Ryan for sheriff." Her phone dinged, signaling a text.

Remembering her message to Conrad, she read over the screen, stiffening.

> Agent Spice: Bennett left town. We can't find him.

CHAPTER EIGHT

Thou shall always note the exits of any building in case you
need to make a speedy escape.

–Jane Ladling's Campaign Companion Code

Thomas Bennett. Missing. The knowledge whirled
through Jane's mind as she and Tiffany drove to
the print shop, picked up the new flyers, then headed to their
meeting with Mrs. Thacker, AKA Jessie...who Jane decided
to refer to as Ms. Jessica. Beau didn't follow them. Or rather,
she didn't see him.

Her knuckles whitened as she gripped the steering wheel.
Had the Gentleman sensed her closing in and killed Tom? Or
had he, maybe, received a threatening letter, like Ashley, and
it sent him running? Or had the bartender slash alleged
ladies' man fled out of guilt or a fear of being caught?

"Well? Did Denise Allen do the dirty deed or not?"
Tiffany demanded from the passenger seat of the hearse.
"That *is* why you risked getting the worst haircut of your life
to question her, yes?"

What! "The worst haircut—"

"I said *risked*, not that you got a hack job. You look amazing. But I only trust my signature locks with Madame LeGrange from Atlanta," the widow said, fluffing said signature locks.

A part of Jane wondered if Tiffany wished the haircut had gone bad. Actually, no. She didn't have to wonder. The widow wasn't that terrible. Perhaps even kind of nice upon occasion. At least Rolex thought so, and he'd always been an excellent judge of character.

Jane sighed. She really needed to bounce ideas off someone. And Tiffany was here. Plus, they'd found the body together. "As you probably guessed, Deputy Gunn was hunting a crime boss here in Aurelian Hills," she began. "He believed Tom was part of the organization. And, according to Denise, maybe even at the top of the organization."

"I can't imagine Tom obeying anyone's orders." Gasping, Tiffany twisted in her seat. Her eyes widened as the rest of her thrummed with excitement. "Jane! What if he's the *leader*?"

"Well, we don't want to get ahead of ourselves," Jane cautioned. But yeah. What if the bartender was, in fact, the Gentleman? Claim you were nothing but an employee while feeding the wrong information to the cops. How better to avoid jail time when the father of one of your many lovers dogged your every step? You not only controlled the evidence, but steered which direction the investigation headed. A brilliant Bond villain level plan. Then, when the deputy learned the truth, you killed him to keep your secret.

Jane immediately booted every other suspect to the second spot on her list, leaving Tom at number one. Thanks to his extracurricular activities with married women, he'd probably taught himself to lie while smiling. He definitely understood how to lead a double life. But most importantly, he comprehended how to sneak in and out of homes undetected.

"He's the leader. I sense it," Tiffany insisted. "Tom Cat could've used his stable of blackmail victims to do his dirty work. Married women are his favorite mark, you see. They never request more, and they keep his secrets so he'll keep theirs. Ask me why I'm sure." Disgust layered her tone.

'How are you su—"

"I didn't mean to literally ask me," the widow interjected. "Good gracious."

Bitterness laced her every timbre. Had Tiff fallen for Tom's charm and gotten burned?

"Before you think I had an affair with Tom Cat," the brunette continued, "I didn't. Kind of. We only kissed. But in my defense, not that I have a defense, Tom paid me a lot of attention when my husband either ignored me or treated me the way my parents did. As if I'm a toy on a shelf, always pristine, perfect and admirable—" She mashed her lips tight, going quiet. Sadness radiated from her. "Well, it doesn't matter now. I was terrified of Marcus finding out about the kiss, so I never stood up for myself when Tom began publicly insulting me."

Jane reached over and squeezed the other woman's hand before she had time to consider her actions. To her surprise, Tiffany didn't rebuff her. Rather, she relaxed into her seat and gave Jane what looked to be a genuine half-smile before gazing out the window and saying, "Tom can spot a vulnerability from miles away. As soon as he does, he pounces."

Jane believed her and yeah, okay, she ached for her too. Everyone carried baggage, didn't they? "My parents considered me a nuisance and left me with Grandma Lily."

"So we're not only cursed in romantic love but in familial love too? Well, that's just great!"

"We aren't cursed?" Jane pursed her lips. She'd meant the

words as a comforting statement, but they had emerged as a hopeful question instead. Trying again. "We aren't cursed." Better. "I used to think we were, so I acted accordingly, thereby cursing myself. A self-fulfilling prophesy, or so I've been told. Recently, I decided to trust Conrad rather than a nothing-but-lies curse. He's rock solid."

Once more, Jane gripped the steering wheel. Her stomach dipped and pitched. She'd just said it. Had opened her mouth and let the insult tumble out. The curse was nothing. It meant nothing. Could do nothing without her help. The realization tumbled through her mind. The curse was no-thing.

"I hope you're right," the other woman muttered.

Jane heard the sentiment she didn't utter: *Otherwise you're destined for the worst heartbreak of your life.* As if by habit, a sense of foreboding swept over her.

No! *Do not give into fear.* That had been her MO for years. If she wanted a different future with Conrad, and she did, she must start making different decisions. And those different decisions started now. Or restarted, since she'd had the same conversation with herself before. But that was the MO of fear—always try to come back.

"You'll see," she promised, surprised by the amount of affection washing through her. Affection. For Tiff. Ugh.

They found a parking space right on Vermeil Street. The cold air stole her breath as they emerged and rushed into the eclectically cozy Treasure Room. A tinkling bell and the sweet scent of vanilla greeted them as they stepped inside. Hannah Thorton, the owner, stood behind the counter, mixing different types of tea leaves.

"Tiff!" Hannah hurried over to hug the brunette, strands of her lovely hair slipping from the loose knot on top of her head. "I just made the most amazing blend. I'm calling it Sweetheart's Delight. Rose petals, dried citrus, and mint with the perfect dash of vanilla." When they parted, she offered Jane a half-smile and a nod. "Miss Ladling."

Jane wouldn't let the cool greeting faze her. After all, the only time she came in lately was to ask questions about a murder. It wasn't her fault when a homicide pointed her in the shop owner's direction.

Tiffany took charge. "As much as I'd enjoy catching up with you, we're here to—"

"See Jessica, I know. Come on. I'll take you back." Hannah led them to a tall bookshelf cluttered with jars of dried tea. With a firm push, a portion of that shelf opened up, revealing—

Jane gawked. "There's a secret room?"

Tiffany crossed the threshold and Jane followed, reeling as she tried to take in everything at once. Bathed in warm light, mystery and intrigue blossomed. Shelves brimming with antique teapots. Delicate cups and saucers lined the walls. The scents of tea, dried flowers and polished wood scented the air. Soft music filtered through the room through unseen speakers, blending with the gentle clinking of a spoon against a porcelain teacup. But the biggest surprise? A window to the other side. Patrons of the secret room had a one-way view into the tearoom. The guests outside had no idea they were being observed. A voyeur's ultimate pleasure. Fascinating and terrifying at the same time.

"I'll leave you to it," Hannah said, closing the door to give them maximum privacy.

A million questions flashed through Jane's mind. How had they kept this secret for so long? Who else knew? Did Hannah accept reservations?

Ms. Jessica occupied one of the Queen Anne chairs at the only table, a stunning piece of furniture with intricate carvings that depicted flowering vines. A ceramic vase the color of a moonlit night graced the center of the table, filled with fresh yellow and pink tulips.

After replacing her teacup in its saucer, Ms. Jessica gracefully rose to her feet. The woman could give lessons in elegance. Her hair was a luxurious chestnut and impeccably styled; no flyaways dared break from the arrangement meticulously framing her face.

"Tiff. Darling. I'm so glad to see you." She kissed the widow's cheeks, one after the other. A glance at Jane dimmed her smile. "And you are?"

"Jane Ladling, ma'am." For some reason, she felt the overwhelming need to curtsey. She nearly pinched the hem of her dress before stopping herself. A blush heated her face. "Yes. Well. I'd welcome some tea, thank you." Gah! Another faux pas. She hadn't been invited. Even still, she sank into a chair at the table and poured herself a cup.

"Yes, please do. This is my own special blend, created by Hannah just for me." Ms. Jessica lowered to her own cushioned chair and studied Jane with narrowing eyes. "You're the cemetery girl who solves crimes."

"Yes. That's me. I refuse to stop until I get answers. So let's get straight to the point." She sipped her drink, blinked, and sipped again. Oh, wow. Tasty! And look. Sponge cakes, scones and clotted cream beckoned her from a small rolling cart. How had she missed those? *Don't mind if I do.* She filled her plate.

Wait. The case! "Did you kill Deputy Gunn to protect your lover, Tom Bennett, from going to jail?"

Tiffany took the seat at Ms. Jessica's side and propped her head on her hands as if she feared what might happen next. "She's kidding. Of course she's kidding."

Ohhhh. Were they playing good cop, scared cop? Because game on!

Ms. Jessica ignored the widow, remaining focused on Jane. "How dare you besmirch my good character." Fury emanated from her. "As if I would ever lower myself to consort with a bartender. If you say otherwise to anyone anywhere, I will sue you for defamation. Do you understand?"

Jane waved her hand, unconcerned. "Feel free. My lawyer would enjoy the deposition." As soon as she found an attorney to represent her for pennies on the dollar. Plus, it would be slander, not defamation. "You have to tell the truth in those things, you know. Now, where was I? Oh yes, perhaps you killed Deputy Gunn because Tom demanded it." She used her most bored tone, taking her bad cop character in a new direction. Cold and hardened. A screw-the-book lawman who'd seen everything and cared for no one. "If he threatened to expose your secret to the whole town, I bet you'd do anything he suggested," Jane continued, slathering blueberry jam over a lemon scone. "Maybe you're actually Tom's boss, the Gentleman. Either way, you might as well confess. Conrad Ryan is on the case, and he always gets his man. And woman. I'm living proof of that."

With a brittle laugh, Tiffany poured herself a glass of tea. Her hands shook. "Guess I won't be invited back."

"You've got that right," Ms. Jessica replied, sitting down her cup before refocusing on Jane. "If that were true, and I'm not saying it is, the same could be said of a dozen other women. So why don't you start with his least favorite ex? Maddie something or other. She phoned and texted him without cease. He called her an obsessed stalker. When he dumped her, she sent him an all caps text telling him he would regret ever being born."

That...hmm. Tom had said he'd broken up with Madeline because he was threatened by her father. Who had told the truth and who had lied? Neither Ms. Jessica nor Tom were trustworthy individuals. She had lied and cheated on her husband, whom she'd vowed to forever love; he blackmailed women he'd previously lured into his bed.

If Ms. Jessica was right, Madeline Gunn could have framed Tom for the murder of her estranged father to ruin his life as promised. She most likely kept a spare key to her father's home. Or Ms. Jessica lied, desperate to protect her secret.

"Did you see the calls and texts, or did he merely tell you about them?" Jane asked.

"Not that you were seeing him," Tiffany added with a wince.

Ms. Jessica gathered her designer purse, settling the strap on her shoulder. "He told. And that's the last I'll ever say on the subject. If you ask me anything else, now or later, if you even mention my name, I'll make you regret it. Good day." Head high, she marched over to press a hidden button on a picture frame.

Jane called, "Vote Conrad Ryan for sheriff!"

The door discreetly clicked open, ending her first and probably only meeting with the first lady of Aurelian Hills.

"One bridge burned. Torched to ash, just like that." Tiffany snapped her fingers. She popped a mini tart into her mouth. "That was awful."

"I mean, was your performance flawless? No. But we got a lead. And sometimes bridges need to be burned." Dang, was Jane getting good at this or what? She drained her teacup, gathered the treats on her plate, plus a few more, then stood. "We're on a roll. To Madeline we go!"

* * *

THANKS TO MADELINE living out loud, Jane easily tracked the "afterlife makeover specialist" to her current location. Her place of employment, Aurelian Hills Cemetery. A shudder ran down Jane's spine.

"The victim's daughter works at a cemetery?" Tiffany demanded as Jane parked in the large lot. Numerous cars filled the area. Today must be a funeral day.

"She does." A terrible one, yes, but finally there was someone who spoke Jane's language.

"I'm tired of dead people," the widow groaned.

"Did you ever think they might be tired of you, too?"

Tiffany humphed. Together, they headed to the main building.

Suddenly Jane remembered all the reasons she disliked the place. Some might call it modest and unobtrusive. She called it a shoebox covered in bricks. Where was the personality? The character? But the worst part had to be the golf cars. Employees drove them across the grounds. On purpose.

Disgusted, Jane entered the reception center. But...hmm. She paused just past the doorway. Was she being watched? Did Beau still track her? Her gaze darted left, right, up, down and behind, but no one seemed to pay her any mind. Least of all Tiffany, who gaped at an empty, open coffin on display.

Focus. With its neutral walls and muted drapery and fixtures, the interior was just as mundane as the exterior. Functional. Subdued. Without a nod to history or understanding of the solemn nature or duty of a caretaker. Except...

Dancing music wafted from somewhere in the back, blending with sporadic cheers and clapping.

Following the sounds, they found Madeline passing out candy hearts near the front counter. The twenty-five year old wore a skintight black gown paired with ebony gloves and tights that looked like cobwebs. Straight, dark hair framed a pale face.

"Welcome to our annual Romancing the Gravestone Valentine's party," Madeline said with a monotone voice, offering each of them a chocolate.

Oh. Right. Valentine's Day kicked off in only three days. Jane had successfully forgotten it again. What was she going to give Conrad? What, what? Seriously. What did you get the man who gave you everything and made you weak in the knees?

"What kind of title is Romancing the Gravestone?" Jane asked with a grimace.

"This is a joke, right?" Tiffany demanded. "You're kidding?"

As someone came from the other direction and opened a door in the back, Jane twisted and turned, attempting to catch a glimpse of the party. Was that—she recoiled in distaste. Strobe lights flashed. Wait staff served finger foods from inside the coffins and guests played what looked to be pinning the toe-tag on the "corpse."

"The owner heard about parties at another cemetery." Madeline hiked her shoulders. "He's trying something new."

Chest puffing with pride—he'd heard about Jane's parties!—she accepted the candy, but only to be polite. The moment she left, the little heart would go straight in the trash where it belonged, along with the rest of Aurelian Hills Cemetery's gimmicks. Such as buy one plot, get the second half off. Or the Don't Move In Too Soon stress ball they once handed out at local businesses.

"I'm investigating the death of your father," Jane said, employing the same respectful tone she used when speaking to mourning families.

Other than a slight shrug, the woman showed zero reaction. "Yeah. So?"

"So. Who is the Forbidden Fruit?" A very mob-like name, now that she thought about it. Very fitting for someone also known as the Gentleman.

"Tom Bennett. Why? You believe he killed my father?"

"Do you?" And why had Madeline offered the name so easily, when she refused to post it?

"As much as I hate him, no. I think he liked the deputy. Even when my father arrested him, Tom hated when I bad-mouthed Dad. He said the guy was kind to him once and an arrest could never stick anyway."

Never stick, huh? Because of the blackmail thing?

"I ache for your loss, by the way," Tiffany piped up softly, as if remembering her manners. "I recently lost my husband."

Madeline scoffed. "I didn't lose anyone. Dad and I had no contact, much less a relationship."

So... Why did a man who seemed to not care about his daughter suddenly start to interfere in her romantic entanglements?

"Are you sure you had no contact?" Jane took a gamble, saying, "Didn't the two of you get together recently and argue about Tom?"

"Yeah. We argued, so what?" the mortician snapped, then neutralized her features.

And the gamble paid off!

Madeline released a heavy breath. "He was never a father to me and suddenly he shows up expecting to tell me who not to date? Not happening. Especially since he was just as bad. A user."

Strong statement. "How did Deputy Gunn use you?"

"He wanted me to warn my online followers about some wannabe kingpin trying to destroy our town or whatever."

Jane's heart leaped. Finally! She was getting somewhere. And yet Madeline's attitude confused her. "But wouldn't giving everyone a warning be a good thing?"

"For all I knew, he hoped to entrap my friends in some kind of sting operation. He'd done it before. As soon as I became a teenager, he hired someone to offer me drugs to see if I'd cave."

Hmm. "Did he give you a name for the kingpin? Or any details at all?" Jane asked.

Madeline looked past her, holding out the bowl to offer a candy to the new arrivals. "Welcome to our annual Romancing the Gravestone Valentine's party." As the pair strutted by them, dressed as *Beetlejuice* characters, the mortician continued, "No, but if I was reading BOSS correctly, he suspected Tom and his brother, or some dark-haired man."

"Boss?" Jane asked. Tom had a brother?

"His Board of Suspects and Shame. It's big and white with wheels."

Like a murder board. Had GBH found it? And who was this dark-haired man? "Any idea where would Tom go to hide if he were in trouble?"

"To whoever is currently paying his bills. A.k.a. his current girlfriend. Who isn't me."

Okay. "Who's his current girlfriend?" Ms. Jessica?

"I have no clue. Ask him."

Tiffany pfted. "As if he'd tell the truth."

"Look, I've told you everything, same as I did with the cops." Madeline placed the bowl on the reception desk. "I've gotta go. I'm the life of the party."

No problem. Jane had things to do, anyway. Like getting ready for dinner at Fiona's and making sense of the thoughts swirling inside her head. "Be sure to vote Conrad Ryan for sheriff," she called as she and Tiffany walked away.

"That didn't go well," her companion muttered once they were secured inside the hearse.

"Something you'll learn as you delve into murder. You

have to deep dive through a lot of lies, opinions, and misdirections to reach the truth."

"And why do we want to do this?"

"We are the only voice the dead have."

CHAPTER NINE

Never pay attention to rumors. They're like always mixed
with assumptions and frosted with exaggerations.

–Jane Ladling's Campaign Companion Code

*W*ith a breakfast casserole in hand, Jane led
Tiffany up Fiona's driveway. The cozy
Bedrock neighborhood provided a blend of southern style
craftsmans and folksy Victorians. Even better, it wasn't far
from Conrad's new place. Perfect for when Jane moved–

Whoa. She may have turned a corner regarding relation-
ships and the curse, but there was no sense in counting her
eggs before they hatched. She had zero plans to permanently
move in with Conrad, now or ever. Garden of Memories was
her sanctuary, and that was that. Wasn't it?

She forced her thoughts to return to her dearest friend.
After Fiona's second husband died, she sold her family farm
outside of town and moved into this charming Victorian.
With its wraparound porch and steeply pitched roof, every-

thing about the place invited new and old friends to relax and enjoy a cup of honey sweetened tea.

They entered the abode without knocking, a privilege granted to Jane years ago. Immediately she was struck by the deluge of whimsy and nostalgia. From the creak of the hardwood floors to old-fashioned lace curtains, every nook and cranny hummed with character. Framed photos of Fiona's children and grandchildren lovingly graced the walls alongside their artwork. Various knitting projects were stashed here and there. The scent of freshly baked chocolate chip cookies lingered in the air.

"This feels like home," Tiffany muttered, eyes wide as she spun in a slow circle, taking everything in. Nervously removing her coat and smoothing her top, she asked, "Who else is coming?"

"Only the members of Team Truth."

"That tells me nothing. Who are the members of Team Truth?"

"Besides Fiona and myself, there's Conrad, Beau, the Sheriff, Trick, Holden and Isaac. Rolex and Cheddar serve as our mascots." *Go guard cat and the corgi!* How cute was that? Maybe she should have matching shirts made.

"Sorry, but my guys can't make it." The masculine voice hit Jane's ears, and she yelped with surprise.

Spinning, she came face to face with a grinning Beau. The stinker must have snuck in behind them, just to prove a point.

"I've got them out on jobs. Also, I told you I can be invisible," he said.

She humphed to let him know such shenanigans were beneath him. "Showing up your boss is a good way to get yourself fired, young man."

He snorted. "You love having me around."

Yeah, she really did. "Do those jobs have anything to do with the current investigation?"

"They do," he replied, but offered no more.

So they were doing what? Guarding Ashley? Searching for Tom? Hunting clues Jane had yet to unearth?

"I'm guessing no one attempted to murder me from the shadows?" Which was kind of a problem. Maybe she wasn't on the right path. After all, the Gentleman had threatened Ashley. So why not Jane? Was she not locked on the right target?

Although, to be fair, the reporter received the letter before Tom left town. What's more, menacing letters took time to create and mail. Maybe Jane's would arrive any day. A girl could hope, anyway. Not that she approved of someone threatening her life. But. With her gut on the fritz, getting a little something to let her know she was on the right track could be nice.

On the other hand, why would a hardened criminal like the Gentleman, who might be cold and cruel enough to sneak into a man's house and dose his morning coffee, run away simply because the law hunted him? Shouldn't he dig in his heels, stand his ground, and wreak more havoc?

And what about Tom's brother? Why had Jane never heard of him? Was Tom's current lady love paying the brother's bills as well?

Something wasn't adding up. What was Jane missing?

Beau snapped his fingers in front of her face, pulling her from her head. "There you are," her friend said with a small smile. "You are correct. No murder attempts. No one but me followed you."

And now she suspected she was on the wrong road again. Unless she wasn't.

Her friend motioned to her hair with a tilt of his chin. "That's new."

"Conrad won't be able to keep his hands out of it," Tiffany piped up with an enthusiastic nod.

"Agreed," Beau said.

Biting her bottom lip and blushing, Jane wound a lock around her index finger. "So you think Conrad will like it?"

"Oh yeah," Beau replied. "He'll like it."

Tiffany brightened and raised an arm into the air. "It was me. I made her do it."

Beau ruffled the *widow's* hair, and she beamed at him. "You entered the bullpen and survived."

"I know!"

Bull? Please. Jane was as sweet as a bird.

The scent of maple syrup, bacon and butter overshadowed the cookies, making her mouth water and her brain blank. She forgot everything but the food. "Fiona?" she called. "We're here, and we're ravenous."

"Come on back," her best friend sang. "The cakes are almost done."

Tiff and Beau followed Jane to the compact kitchen, which Fiona had remodeled before moving in, adding new stainless steel appliances and a farmhouse sink. The cabinets she'd painted a cheery buttercup.

The widow hurried past her to reach Fiona first and claim a hug, clinging to the other woman as if she were a lifeline. "I'm so glad to see you."

"I'm glad to see you, too, hon," Fiona replied, patting her.

Understanding and compassion consumed Jane. Was Tiffany lonely? The socialite had lost her husband, her fiancé, and then her friends. Maybe, just maybe, Jane could be part of the healing process. A support rather than a hindrance to healing. Give the widow a chance to grow in light rather than wither in darkness. Maybe, if they let themselves, they could be blessed in the familial love department.

GENA SHOWALTER & JILL MONROE

Her cell phone dinged, snagging her attention. She checked the screen.

> Agent Spice: Sweetheart, this is one of the most difficult messages I've ever sent, but I have to miss pancake night. I will, however, pick you up from Fiona's as soon as I'm free. To make amends, I'll come bearing fresh information about the case...

Shivers cascaded over her. A smile blooming, Jane shot him a reply:

> Perhaps I'll share what I learned, too. But only after I get a kiss hello. And many compliments about my new haircut.

> Agent Spice: Are you even more adorable?

She opted to accept his compliment and tease him.

> Jane: Probably! If such a thing is even possible.

> Agent Spice: It is. I've watched you do it every day that I've known you.

Her smile returned, only bigger, and she hugged her cell to her chest. This man just got her.

She wanted this case solved quickly, so they could march into their future. Conrad, becoming sheriff. Jane, his forever girlfriend, who discovered what life had in store for her.

All right. No more mushy stuff. She turned her thoughts to the case. Specifically what she'd learned from Madeline Gunn. Tom Bennett might be the Gentleman, who possibly staying with a former lover rather than a current one. Jane's reason for thinking so was simple. The guy relied on blackmail to get what he wanted, not affection, hard work, and trust. He'd go where he felt safest: the person with the most to lose if their affair were discovered.

Was that Jessica Thacker? The fury she'd displayed could only spring from fear.

"Where's Conrad?" Fiona asked as she and Tiffany finally parted.

"He can't make it, so it's just gonna be us and the sheriff," Jane said, going over to get *her* hug from Fiona.

The older woman turned pensive. "Our men gotta be working on something big, because Raymond can't make it, either."

Well. "That is the price we pay for dating such dedicated smokeshows."

"That it is." Dark eyes sparkling, Fiona chucked her under the chin and waved her to the table. "Show the others to the dining room. The hot cakes are ready to serve."

"Yes, ma'am." Jane led the way to a spacious dining room that displayed a vintage sideboard, AKA Fiona's most cherished heirloom. Their little trio sank onto the enchantingly mismatched chairs that surrounded a large, rustic farmhouse table.

Delicate china, freshly polished silverware, and linens molded into swans decorated each place setting. Fiona didn't believe in leaving the good stuff for special occasions. Fine dinnerware was meant to be used. She entered with a heaping platter of food, set it on the table, and sank into the spot at the head. Everyone dug in. Jane savored every bite as her taste buds exploded with flavor.

"Oh my gosh," Tiffany exclaimed. She wiped syrup from her chin. "This is amazing!" She shoveled in another bite, then another, until little beads of maple dripped from the corners of her mouth. "I want these every day for the rest of forever!"

"Ladling blood is definitely flowing through your veins," Beau said, his amusement clear. "In grade school, Jane waxed poetic about these pancakes at almost every lunch."

Fiona nodded in understanding. "I believe it. Not a day has gone by without a request for pancakes. Even if she only asks with her eyes."

"Because these pancakes are a gift from above, and everyone everywhere should agree, no matter their bloodline," Jane exclaimed.

Tiffany was too busy eating to offer her agreement.

"Do you know how to knit, Tiffany?" Fiona asked out of the blue.

The widow shook her head, saying, "No," with a mouthful of pancake. "Never tried it." In went another bite.

"Well, no worries. We'll teach you. Won't we Jane?"

"Sure," she said, the word muffled since she, too, had a mouthful of pancake.

Her friends shared a good laugh. But Fiona sobered all too soon, telling them, "Some women at the senior center were discussing a dangerous street thug, the Gentleman. Pepper heard from Martha, who heard from her daughters, Athena and Amelia, who heard from their cousin Zoey that a gal named Noel heard he was dangerous.'"

"Who is this Noel?" Someone Jane needed to interview?

"She's from Atlanta."

The info had spread to the city, then.

"Ashley Katz posted on the *Headliner*," Beau said. "She asked citizens to message her with any dealings they've had with a quote unquote cartel of criminals and their twisted leader, who dared leave our town with a murder house."

"Murder House," Jane echoed. Not a bad name for the place. But perhaps she needed to speak with the reporter again. Find out what she'd learned.

"I'm considering buying and flipping the deputy's house."

Beau finished off his sweet tea. "Maybe the Clayton Board-inghouse, too."

Tiffany gasped and shook her head. "No. Absolutely not. That boarding house is super mega haunted."

"Rumors have swirled since before I was born," Fiona informed him. "Sometimes I forget that even though you're from here, you moved early, leaving gaps in your Aurelian Hills education."

Jane put down her fork and sighed. "I'm sorry to say this, but Beau, don't listen to them. No place in Aurelian Hills is haunted. Believe me, I've basically lived my whole life on the grounds of a cemetery and I've seen zero ghosts."

"Well then, you willing to spend a night alone in the old boarding house?" Fiona challenged with a wave of her fork.

Jane pictured the dilapidated home and swallowed. "No. But only because the roof might cave in!"

"Or because you sense how angry the ghosts are, just like the rest of us," Tiffany said with a shudder.

Beau leaned against his chair. "Well, don't keep me in suspense. What's the story?"

Fiona got more comfortable. "During the early 1920s, the widow Hattie Clayton operated the town's only boarding-house, with a surprisingly high death rate."

"Men checked out, but sometimes only in a body bag," Tiffany added, getting into the retelling. "They traveled for work, rented a room for fun, or came for a holiday with their wife, and no matter how healthy and happy they appeared walking in, they suffered from a heart attack or committed suicide."

Jane made a skeptical noise in the back of her throat. "Has anyone actually found any documents to support these claims?"

Fiona held up her hands. "Today, some people consider Miss Clayton one of the most prolific serial killers in the

United States. See, Hattie was known as what my grandma referred to as a Helper Woman."

Tiffany leaned forward. "As in, she helped you lose your husband real fast. Six feet under fast."

Beau nodded his understanding. "Go on."

"I just want to interject that many of those husbands, boyfriends, fathers and family members are buried at the Garden and nary a one has lodged a complaint," Jane said.

"Rumors suggested Hattie was the woman to go to when a male gave you a hard time and you hoped to make him disappear. Boom! Death!" Fiona clapped her hands for emphasis. "No one knows if she did the deeds herself or aided the afflicted women. The secret endures to this day."

"What happened to Miss Clayton?" Beau asked. "And why did guys keep staying with her?"

"Bragging rights maybe?" Fiona wrinkled her nose. "Ultimately, townsfolk banded together to bring her to justice. She holed up within the walls of the boarding house until the mob ripped the front door off its hinges. Within minutes, she fell out a window and died upon impact. Nobody knows if she was pushed or jumped to avoid a trial, but the place has been haunted by her and her victims ever since and left abandoned."

"That explains the cheap price and extended listing," Beau said. "Or *formally* so cheap. Suddenly I'm in a bidding war with another potential buyer."

Fiona clucked her tongue. "Must be an outsider."

Tiffany flattened her hands against the table. "As lovely as the talk of vengeful ghosts isn't, how about we focus on something pleasant?" She filled her plate with three more pancakes. "I'll go first. What did you get Conrad for Valentine's Day, Jane?"

Jane's blood flashed ice cold in an instant. She shot a

worried glance at Beau, who shrugged all too innocently. "I... uh...well..."

"Oookay. I'll take that to mean you've gotten him nothing, and have no idea where to start." The widow drenched her cakes in butter and syrup.

"I have ideas." Listing things off the top of her head, she said, "A homemade book with coupons to redeem for his favorite foods and such. Although, he can have my dishes and desserts for free so maybe a cheese of the month club instead. Who doesn't like cheese? Or a bird, to add to our growing menagerie."

"Brilliant idea incoming!" Tiffany dove into her hot stack, saying, "Why don't you give him a promise ring with your name engraved in the band? That kind of gesture always made me go weak in the knees. I know a guy who can get you the finest metal and do the engraving in less than a day."

A promise ring. Not a bad idea, actually. She longed to be his forever Valentine. But dang it, that title—Valentine—still didn't satisfy whatever desire frothed within Jane. A yearning for...more. More Conrad. More commitment. More *everything*. But, but... The curse.

Could she risk his life? *Would* she risk his life? The nothing curse had no power without fear.

Let fear win the most important battle of all?

"I'm on a budget," Jane said. "Unless I throw together a new event at the Garden. The premiere event planners in town are practically *begging* me to get something on the books." Well, the sisters had sent a text a few weeks ago, wanting to know if she would agree to host another town game night. "Problem is, I'm smack dab in the middle of a murder investigation and a campaign."

"I made Raymond a sweater with his favorite color yarn," Fiona said, dabbing at her mouth with a lace-trimmed napkin. "Make Conrad something he'll like. A pillow, perhaps. A nice square with soft padding that will remind him of you every time he sleeps."

Another excellent idea. And yet... it wasn't quite it. "We haven't heard from you, Beau. What do men like to receive from their womenfolk?"

Both Fiona and Tiffany zoomed their gazes to the only male in the room, instantly captivated and awaiting his response.

He froze with his fork halfway to his mouth. "Trust me. You don't want to hear my opinion."

"Oh, but we do," Fiona insisted, eyes twinkling.

"Yes, yes," Tiffany said with an exaggerated nod.

"We like...things." Cheeks pinkening, he shoveled a mouthful of Jane's casserole into his mouth, then chewed and chewed and chewed, unable to speak.

No matter. They waited patiently, staring at him.

Finally he swallowed. "You should probably move on to someone or something else." He shoveled in another bite, ensuring he couldn't speak again.

When Jane's phone rang, Beau burst out, "Thank the good Lord."

She was snickering as she checked the screen. Huh. NewsKat. Had another letter arrived? Maybe a witness had emerged after she'd posted her article.

Jane held up a finger, the universal sign for "I need a minute," then stepped away from the table. "Hello?"

"Jane, this is Ashley Katz." Dread and worry coated the words.

"What's going on?" Her stomach turned inside out. "Is something wrong?"

"I'm sorry to tell you this, but Mr. Ryan was shot. He's at Pinetum Regional now."

CHAPTER TEN

Thou shall never let your boyfriend wear anything other than his campaign T-shirt, even if it's freezing outside.

–Jane Ladling's Campaign Companion Code

*J*ane's stomach churned with sickness. The second Beau parked his truck in the hospital's lot, she shoved open the passenger door and ran, her flats slamming against the pavement.

"Look both ways," he called.

She knew Fiona and Tiffany arrived in Fiona's convertible because they called for her, too. But she didn't stop, just kept motoring forward, zooming past the electronic doors and into the Emergency Room. The last time she'd been here, she'd visited Sheriff Moore after his heart attack. He'd come out better on the other side, and Jane prayed her boyfriend experienced the same results.

"Conrad Ryan," she shouted far too loudly.

The bespeckled man behind the reception desk conveyed

only sympathy. He probably dealt with distressed family and friends daily.

Jane moderated her volume. "Conrad Ryan's room, please."

Barrow came striding around a corner, spotted her, and halted. He projected confusion and resolve as she rushed over.

"Where is he?" she demanded, cold all over. "How is he?"

The big man heaved a sigh. "He's fine. He'll mend. Come on. I'll take you to him."

They navigated the hallways, passing curtained off rooms. Jane's knees shook. Conrad was fine. He would mend. That was great. Wonderful. She still needed to see him. "What happened?"

"I'll let him explain." Barrow pushed aside a privacy curtain, allowing her to enter the space first.

And there he was. Conrad Ryan. The love of her life. Her breath caught. He was indeed her love, wasn't he? The man she adored with every fiber of her being. There was no use denying it anymore. No forgetting it. No hiding it. He was perfectly imperfect and wonderful and vibrant and brilliant and funny and, and, and...Tears filled her eyes, her vision blurring. Her bottom lip trembled.

The love of her life sat at the edge of the gurney, shirtless, with smears of dried blood on his muscular chest. Locks of dark hair stuck out in spikes. He strained to slip a suit jacket over his shoulders. One of those shoulders was wrapped with white gauze. Pain marred his beautiful features.

Maybe she whimpered. Maybe he sensed her. His gaze flipped up. He did a double take.

"I like your hair."

"Where's your shirt? Never mind, I have a campaign T-shirt in my car."

They spoke nonsense in unison. He jumped from the bed

and reached out with his bandaged arm, winced, then reached with the other. Jane raced into his embrace, careful to avoid his injury.

He kissed the top of her head. "I'm fine. The bullet grazed me. Got a couple stitches so I'm good to go. The shirt's in the trash, by the way."

"Apologies," Barrow said from the doorway.

Conrad clutched her tighter, glaring from his former partner to the sheriff, who sat in the corner. "I told you not to call her."

"And I heeded your demand," the sheriff countered. "Despite my better judgment. Thanks to you, I'm due a tongue lashing from Fiona."

Jane sniffled and pulled away to prop her hands on her hips. "You planned to hide your wound from me?"

Conrad winced. "Not hide. I planned to tell you face to face, so you'd see I was fine."

"No. That is completely unacceptable and not at all what partners do. So get this straight," she said, poking him in the chest and only caring the slightest bit when he hissed. "I'm here for the long haul, and we share everything. You don't pick and choose what's good for me like I'm a child. We decide things together. Got it?"

Surprise lit his baby blues. "I…yes. Okay. You're right."

"Of course I am." And dang it, she cared big time about his pain level. "Did I hurt you?" She petted and kissed the spot she'd jabbed.

His fingers closed around her hand, engulfing it with his warmth. "The little twinge was worth it to hear your impassioned speech."

"What happened?" she asked, finally warming up.

"I'll explain, I promise. Will you tell me how you found out I was here?"

"Ashley called me." And. Hmm. How had the other

woman known that no one else would phone Jane to give her the lowdown? "Ashley Katz from the Headliner."

"Reporters," Conrad grumbled.

She burrowed her face in the hollow of his neck, tears welling in her eyes once more. "You could have died," she mumbled. Then words poured from her without a breath in between. "What if this is the curse in action? I mean, I linked our names together on the flyer. That was practically a nuclear bomb."

"Breathe," he said, petting her hair, and she did.

In. Out. She'd planned on not giving the curse any power, she really had, but old habits died hard and this was too coincidental.

"Give us some privacy," he said.

"Things were just getting good," the sheriff grumbled. He stood and ambled past the curtain, taking a willing Barrow with him.

Conrad cupped one side of her face and traced his thumb over the rise of her cheek. Features alight with tenderness, he said, "I think you're right. This is the curse in action."

Wait. What? "You told me the curse didn't exist!" she squeaked. "You're supposed to disagree with me and assure me everything is going to be okay. Why aren't you assuring me everything is going to be okay?"

"No, sweetheart. I told you there was a curse because you believed it, and I stand by that. The curse was conceived with a thought, nurtured, birthed, and grown to full maturity. It lives and breathes in you, and it knows it's losing its hold. Now it's fighting back, doing its best to convince you to follow its lead so it can strengthen again."

That kind of sort of made sense. The curse had ruled her family for so long. Too long. And she'd allowed it. For all of her life, she'd nursed, petted, and humored it. Even after she'd committed to Conrad, she'd held a part of herself back from him, clinging to the curse.

"I know you're afraid," he continued. "But I need you to trust me rather than the curse." His gaze roved over her face and canted his head. "Did you cut your hair for the case?"

"Tiffany insisted." She played with the ends. "But you like it?"

A smile bloomed, his irises glittering with delight. As his lids hooded, he shifted a lock between his fingers. "I don't think I've ever liked anything more. Please do not run away or ice me out, keeping me from this perfection."

A blush seared twin circles into her cheeks. "I won't, I promise." But she did need to consider some things. She'd basically shouted that she wasn't leaving him. Did she have the courage to follow through?

Solve the case, figure it out. This investigation was personal now. No one hurt her man.

"Well? What happened? I demand every detail, beginning with how much you hated leaving without me this morning."

He snort-laughed. "I've been discharged. Let's go to the cafeteria and talk."

"Is there a reason you keep delaying the question?" she asked with a prim tone.

"Yes." He took her hand and ushered her into the hall. They strode past the sheriff and Barrow, who huddled together, talking.

Curiosity frothed within her. She and Conrad reached the cafeteria, a comfortable space for visitors and staff to dine. After purchasing drinks, Jane steered them to a secluded table in the farthest corner of the room, the seats a muted, soothing sea foam. No man's land.

He sat across from her and clasped her hand again. "Here's what happened. Leaving you tucked safe and warm at home was tough, but somehow, I had to do to make a meeting with Barrow. We checked alibis, questioned people of interest, and went over evidence. Tests came back, and many of the hairs discovered at the deputy's house were cut rather than shed or pulled. But those with roots belonged to eighteen different people. Most notably Denise Allen, the hairdresser ex, Madeline Gunn, the daughter, and Ashley Katz, our fellow file member. We also spoke with Mr. Garfield. When I heard a noise in back, I branched off to investigate. I was shot as I rounded a corner."

A crime of panic or an act the killer pre-planned? "Was the shooter a man? Woman?"

"I caught the barest glimpse of him from behind. Tall and lean, with dark hair. He used a forty-caliber pistol with a suppressor. The same type of gun on the deputy's walls."

Definitely connected to the case. If someone was shooting at Conrad, then he must be on the right track. But that meant Jane was on the right track, too, and so far nothing.

Tall and lean with dark hair described Tom Bennett to a tee. Also the mysterious dark haired man Madeline mentioned. "Did you receive a warning letter before the attack?"

"I did not."

So... Her thoughts raced a mile a minute, jumping from here to there. "To know the hairs belonged to specific people, you needed to compare two samples. Which means they were in the system. And why did he possess all that hair?" She recalled the pile she'd seen at the Gilded Scissor Salon. "What if the deputy visited his former girlfriend and bagged up a handful of strands? Or maybe Denise gave him a bag." Eww. But why do such a thing? Why *want* such a thing?

"The current theory is that there is no theory," he said and sighed.

"Yes. I concur," Jane muttered, her gut remaining silent.

"As for your other questions," Conrad said, "Deputy Gunn had digital files on Allen and Katz with tests run by a private lab he paid for with personal money. He didn't have a file on his daughter, but we did. When she lived in Atlanta, she spent several months behind bars for drug possession with intent to sell."

Whoa! Madeline had sold drugs? Perhaps even the exact drugs Tom was arrested for having? More evidence that pointed to the ex-boyfriend being the Gentleman. Or, perhaps, a certain family member... Like his brother.

Tom may have dated Madeline with hopes of recruiting her into his brother's top secret organization. Because an absent sibling could absolutely be the Gentleman. One brother called the shots, the other did the work.

An opposite theory suggested Gunn confiscated drugs from his daughter and framed Tom.

Jane would start with the brother. "Madeline Gunn told me Tom has a sibling."

"Yes. Oliver Bennett. Ollie. He died three years ago in a car accident." Sympathy threaded Conrad's tone. He understood the pain of losing your family in a wreck. "Thomas Bennett drove the vehicle, and Deputy Gunn worked the case. The deputy's notes assign no blame to the younger Bennett. The car spun out of control on ice and hit a pole. Other than a few casual run ins, nothing suggests Gunn and Thomas Bennett maintained a relationship afterward. Well, until the CI thing came up. But I digress. We think Thomas lied to Miss Gunn, pretending that his sibling still lived in order to use the deceased Mr. Bennett as an excuse to spend time with other marks."

"Possible. But why did Deputy Gunn add Oliver to BOSS? Board of Suspects and Shame, according to Madeline Gunn. The deputy had access to the same databases you do and knew the other Bennett boy was dead."

He shrugged. "Right now, we don't know if there *is* a BOSS. We've found no sign of its existence."

"Maybe he kept it in a storage facility?"

"If so, there's no financial record of renting one."

"Relocated it?"

"Or destroyed it."

Well. How disappointing. Perhaps Madeline had lied. Or had the authorities overlooked it? "I'm happy to search the house. I'm as great at finding hidden treasures as I am at homicide investigations. Just ask the little boy who lost his smile. Took me twenty-four hours, but I helped him find it."

A bemused expression passed over Conrad's face. "Is that little boy Beau?"

Affection squeezed Jane's chest. "Yes. And as you have clearly witnessed, he still has it."

Conrad snorted. "I'll do my best to get you approved for a tour of the house."

"Thank you, thank you, thank you. Oh! Before I forget, Madeline thinks Tom is hiding with his girlfriend, who might be Jessica Thacker."

"As far as we can tell, Mr. Bennett and Mrs. Thacker ended things. He's already seeing other women." Conrad traced his thumb over her knuckles. "Tomorrow, we'll be interviewing the mayor. He might have known about the affair and feared Deputy Gunn would expose the truth, hurting his reputation and pride."

"An act of revenge." But oh, boy, did Conrad and crew have a mountain to climb with the whole Thacker situation. If the husband mirrored the wife, he would deny, deny, deny. "For the record, I disagree with Madeline. Lovers can turn on you. I think he's staying with someone he's blackmailing. Perhaps Jessica." But. Hmm. "What if *the mayor* is the Gentleman? Madeline said her father suspected Tom Bennett, plus his brother and a dark-haired man. The mayor has salt and pepper hair, heavy on the pepper, ergo a dark-haired man. Maybe I should attend the interrogation? For the good of the case, of course."

He snorted. "I'll see what I can do."

Jane's heart leaped. "What did you ask Mr. Garfield about?"

"His children." Conrad released her to take a drink of his sweet tea. "They both visit often, and either one or both could have snuck into the deputy's home."

The Garfield siblings. Ken and Barbie. They *did* have a motive. Finally settle the tree debate between neighbors. Even as cantankerous as Hugh Garfield was, the pair probably loved him. And, with his illness, stress must be especially bad for his health.

"Were you able to speak with the children themselves?" she asked. "Does Ken have dark hair?"

"No and yes. But if I had to guess, I'd say Bennett is my shooter. He was either hiding in the Garfield house or lurking nearby."

Then Tom was going down. But what did Conrad's attempted murder add up to? That Tom was, in fact, the Gentleman, rather than the mayor or his brother, who Gunn might have suspected still lived, if BOSS actually existed? And if so, how did they prove it?

CHAPTER ELEVEN

Thou shall always trust your boyfriend to get the job done,
but never be afraid to doublecheck his work.

–Jane Ladling's Campaign Companion Code

"*Y*ou're taking the day off, and that's an order."
Jane used the sternest tone she could manage as
she keyed into Conrad's home.

As soon as they were inside, he gathered her close with
his good arm. She leaned into the touch. "I really am okay,"
he said.

Mercilessly, she pointed to the couch. "You are allowed to
do nothing but relax and heal. Am I understood?"

He laced his fingers through hers. "As long as you're
doing it with me, I will obey Madame Jane."

All day snuggling with Conrad? Well. Sacrifices must be
made. Nodding, she announced, "Fine. But only after I get
you properly settled in."

She helped him settle on the cushions, and Conrad
soaked up the attention like a sponge. Propped on pillows

and stretched out, he watched her with soft eyes as she removed his shoes, tucked a blanket around him, and sat beside him to smooth the hair from his brow.

"You're taking this so much better than I expected," he said, leaning over to brush the tip of his nose against hers.

Had she run from him in the past, any time the curse seemed poised to strike? Yes. Would she run in the future? The urge might be there, but she'd fight it. Right now, she concentrated solely on his recovery.

"I wonder if we should send out a press release to let the citizens know you took a bullet for them," she muttered thoughtfully. More to herself than Conrad. "Yes. We should. I'll contact Ashley." Perhaps, once the conversation got going, she'd ask the burning question. *How did you know?*

She grabbed her phone and noticed another text from June. Oops! Jane had forgotten to respond to her sister's last text.

> Juniverse: What are you up to?

As much curious as remorseful, Jane responded:

> Patching up my boyfriend. What are YOU up to?

> Juniverse: Nothing.

Oookay.

> Jane: Is there something you'd like to discuss?

> Juniverse: No thanks.

Sighing, Jane shot off a quick query to NewsKat to get things rolling, but minutes passed and nothing came in. She set the phone aside and noticed Conrad giving her a bemused look. "What?"

"This is you taking a day off?" He pulled her next to him, and she let him, both of him careful of his injury.

They cuddled up and spent hours chatting about everything and nothing. Even Cheddar hopped onto the couch with them. In between topics, Conrad fielded calls from Wyatt and his favorite foster mom, Susan. Both asked- to speak with Jane. Only her assurances that the big, bad lawman was on the mend, thanks to her tender care, helped alleviated their worries.

The only downside was Rolex's refusal to participate in the layabout. Instead, he perched in a window seat, peering out the glass longingly. Missing Tiffany?

Conrad's stomach grumbled as the sun lowered on the horizon, and Jane shot up. Someone was hungry? Under her watch? Grandma Lily and Fiona would be scandalized. "You require nourishment to speed up your recovery, and I will provide it."

"Just order pizza or something," Conrad said, trying to draw her back into his tempting warmth.

What Conrad wanted, Conrad got—except that. She clucked her tongue. "As if I will feed you something made by other people while your very life hangs in the balance. Clearly you don't understand basic pampering."

She handed him the TV remote, stood, and aimed for the kitchen. It was time someone put their stamp on the functional workspace. Of course, she didn't have any of her recipe cards, but she could make a few things from memory. Since Conrad had over-stocked the pantry in anticipation of her arrival, she had all the necessary ingredients for a feast of Conrad's favorites. Even dishes he didn't yet know he loved. Chicken fried steak and gravy, shrimp and grits, red beans and rice, chicken and dumplings, peach cobbler, cranberry and marshmallow salad, and okra soup.

As she cooked, fear attempted another takeover. Conrad was okay today, but what happened tomorrow? She couldn't keep him locked in his home forever. Would the shooter strike again?

She fought back with the best weapon: truth. She could and would learn the assailant's identity, even if she had to cross lines and cut through red tape.

So. What had she learned so far? Deputy Gunn possessed a plethora of hair most likely obtained from his ex-girl-friend's salon. Said ex-girlfriend may or may not have known of it. He'd conducted private DNA testing on multiple strands, as if searching for someone in particular. Madeline Gunn had spent time in prison. Ashley Katz was hardcore working the case, as evidenced by her phone call to Jane. Conrad hadn't received a letter warning him of impending doom before the shooting, which wasn't the Gentleman's MO. If the Gentleman was the killer. Which he might or might not be.

What mattered? What didn't?

Maybe she should start at the beginning. She spotted the small magnetic whiteboard on Conrad's refrigerator, and her fingers twitched. It wasn't as good as her rollaround board at home, but it would do. Anything to help her organize her thoughts. As she waited for the rice to boil, Jane quickly jotted down outstanding questions:

- Deputy Gunn's evidence of organized crime in Aurelian Hills?
- Why hide his suspicions from SM?
- Why gather DNA data? Distrust of coworkers or a need to hide his own actions?

"We know Sheriff Moore isn't bought," Conrad said, plopping on a bar stool. "He's one of the most upright people I've ever worked with."

"Agreed." Raymond Moore was honest to a fault, loyal to the max, and as stubborn as steel. "Perhaps the deputy believed a lie someone told him about the sheriff."

"Perhaps. Gunn once accused Raymond of accepting bribes. He was unable to prove it. An internal investigation concluded with unwavering support for the sheriff."

"Interesting. But what are you doing in here? You're supposed to be resting on the couch," she scolded.

He shrugged his uninjured shoulder. "It's boring in there without you. I can rest right here and watch you cook."

She couldn't very well argue with a wounded lawman who desired to spend time with her, now could she? And since he wasn't going anywhere, she might as well make use of him. "What about the rest of the deputies? Are they trustworthy? I went to school with some of them, and quite a few tried to cheat off my homework."

"Barrow and I looked into the other deputies. They checked out. Considering Raymond was in the process of documenting complaints against Gunn, we figure the deputy learned of it and hoped to strike first."

Wow. Suspicious much? If the others were on the up and up, Deputy Gunn had no reason to avoid sharing case information unless he had something to hide. "Have you ever paid out of pocket for an outside lab to run tests?"

Conrad shook his head. "I've had no need for private testing. But also, some tests are pricey."

So why had Deputy Gunn forked over the cash?

Her thoughts turned to the last item on her just-learned list. Tom's dead brother, Oliver. Was there a chance he'd faked his death? "Was the brother positively identified before burial or cremation? Does he look anything like Thomas?"

She slid a small bowl of shrimp and grits Conrad's way, along with a spoon.

"Oliver died in the hospital. From the photos we've seen, they shared similarities, but many more differences."

With so many hospital staff involved and more differences than similarities, there'd been no faking his death. Probably. Not with any ease. Although, a person didn't have to look anything like him to steal his identity—no, that wasn't likely either. GBH would have noticed if Oliver's name and social security number were used. Unless it was being saved for a coming change of identity. A smooth switch from, say, a murderous Tom Cat to an innocent Oliver? The bartender might have feared the deputy stumbling upon the information. A reason to strike hard and fast.

Dang. Things were not looking good for Tom. Every time Jane turned around, something new pointed to his guilt. So why wasn't she satisfied with the explanation? Where was her gut when she needed it most?

"Let's backtrack to Deputy Gunn and his files," she said, stirring the beans. "You mentioned Sheriff Moore documenting Gunn's screw ups."

"More and more of his arrestees were claiming a set up. The very reason Raymond recommended me for sheriff rather than his own employee."

"Also because you're amazing."

"Well, that too. But his endorsement apparently infuriated Deputy Gunn."

The timer on the stove rang, indicating the peach cobbler was done. Perfect timing. The dessert would cool as they ate other dishes that were ready to devour.

Instead of placing the food on the sideboard as she had with yesterday's breakfast, she served from the countertop, spooning a little bit of everything onto Conrad's plate.

As she settled in beside him, he said, "This is our day off.

From this moment on, we are two normal people without a single care. No murder investigation. No campaign. Okay?"

Normal. She could do normal. Jane stored her mental case files and cleaned the office in her mind, then beamed a smile at the man she'd only just realized she loved beyond reason. A shock among shocks she had yet to fully process. "Okay."

But what did normal people discuss?

Oh! Without case details crowding her brain, she recalled the errand he'd run the morning Deputy Gunn died. Had Conrad, perhaps, done something special for Valentine's Day? The most magnificent and wonderful and horrifying of gestures because she still hadn't figured out the perfect gift for him. "We can describe our ideas for Valentine's Day. You will go first, of course."

"Of course," he deadpanned before one of those soft, adoring smiles lifted the corners of his beautiful mouth. "I'm thinking we'll have dinner and exchange gifts."

She gulped. How was she supposed to glean any helpful information from such a vague answer? "Yes. Um. Sounds good." But what was she supposed to do about his gift, dang it?

❧ ❧ ❧ ❧

JANE WAS STILL INTERNALLY agonizing over the gift the next morning as she stood behind a two-way mirror, gazing into an interrogation room, Sheriff Moore beside her.

Hugh Garfield and his lawyer, Barbie Garfield-Johnson, sat on one side of a table. She wore a charcoal suit paired with a lovely lavender silk top. Her shoulder-length brown hair framed a pretty face. Cat eyeglasses completed her look, rendering her the picture of professional sophistication.

In strode Barrow and Conrad, and Barbie's jaw went slack. To Jane's amazement, her boyfriend looked no worse for wear after being shot. He wore his usual suit, his bandage hidden beneath his shirt. His color was good, his motions mostly smooth. The biggest difference, he hadn't shaved. A thicker than usual shadow complimented his strong jaw, and oh, did he knock her socks off.

But she wasn't here to ogle him. Their day off had ended. Now they worked to solve the case and save her man. If the shooter tried again...

Jane balled her hands into fists. *I will burn this world to the ground!* After she saved the mascots and members of Team Truth, of course. And maybe Tiffany too. Possibly a handful of others. But no more than that! She'd also salt the land where the culprit lived.

Conrad and Barrow made introductions before settling in at the other side of the table.

"That boy loves you, you know," the sheriff said, after sipping his cup of coffee.

It was as if her heartbeat skidded to a halted before pounding into a sprint.

"If you're going to dump him because of some foolish notion that you're doomed," her companion added, "do it sooner rather than later."

Her gaze strayed to Conrad's handsomely rugged face. Warmth spread through her chest. She swallowed the lump growing in her throat. "I'm not dumping him because of the curse." She aimed for a neutral tone, but her words came out like a promise. Time to change the subject. "When will they start?"

"Soon. Those GBH agents have a number of tactics up their sleeve, and delay is one of them," the sheriff replied. "Most people can't bear it."

A full minute passed before Barbie cracked. "You're wasting our time."

Finally Conrad spoke up. "Let's get to it then. Tell me about your relationship with Thomas Bennett."

"I told you," the elder Garfield griped before his daughter could stop him. "I have no relationship with the guy. I don't even know who that is."

"I wasn't addressing you," the former special agent said with a cold smile Jane never wished to receive. "I'm talking to you, Ms. Garfield-Johnson."

The younger Garfield blinked rapidly. Oh snap. Had Barbie been a victim of Tom Cat?

Would she spin a story laden with excuses or clam up like the mayor's team? Earlier, Conrad had interviewed the mayor, his wife, and their three lawyers. But they'd said little and revealed nothing before leaving.

Mr. Mayor had been informed of his wife's alleged affair, but he'd defended her without batting an eye. Had he already known and worked to cover it up?

"You were once a regular at the Gold Star Lounge, yes?" Conrad continued. "You had dealings with Mr. Bennett."

The attorney gulped, her eyes wide. "I might have ordered drinks from him. What does that have to do with anything?"

Such obvious feigned ignorance. A practiced barrister should be smoother.

"Mr. Bennett is a person of interest in an ongoing murder investigation," Barrow explained. "He's also a prime suspect for a number of other felonies. Including the attempted murder of a federal agent. Anyone who harbors such an individual will face the same charges."

The color drained from Ms. Garfield-Johnson's face. She licked her lips. "What if, hypothetically, my client didn't know he harbored such a man inside his house?"

Father Garfield gave his only daughter a double take.

"You snuck in another boy?"

"Shut up, Dad," Barbie said before laughing nervously. "If I can give you Tom Bennett, does this go away for me and my father? No one else needs to hear of it?"

Well, well, well. Barbie Garfield-Johnson was a married woman who Tom Bennett had slept with and then blackmailed. The attorney must have helped the bartender to keep word of their affair from reaching her husband. A truth Tom had used to his advantage to hide out in her father's house.

"I can't promise that," Barrow said. "I may need to speak with your husband. But I can promise you there's a hundred percent chance others will know if you withhold any information from us."

A beat of silence. "Step outside, dad," Barbie commanded, her tone firm.

Mr. Garfield's mouth opened and closed, but eventually he wheeled his oxygen tank out of the room. The moment the door sealed shut behind him, Barbie launched into her story. "Yeah, I messed up. My marriage was on the rocks, and there was Tom, pouring drinks and encouraging me to share. I don't think my husband had really listened to me in a year, but Tom did." She jabbed her finger against the tabletop. "I went home with him. A few weeks later, I reconciled with my husband. He stepped up, and we've never been happier. That's when Tom showed up with a video featuring our night together." Running out of steam, shoulders slumping, she dropped her head into her hands. "I can't believe how stupid I was."

Jane tapped her toe against the linoleum floor. Standard cheater stuff. *Hurry up and spill the deets.*

Barrow leaned forward. "Was he staying in your father's home?"

"Yes. Tom demanded I make it happen, or threatened to post the footage on the *Headliner*. I'd never be able to show my face in this town again. Who's gonna hire the philanderer with a sex tape to represent them? Can you imagine?" Barbie wrung her hands together on the tabletop. "You see? I had no other choice but to help him."

"How did you explain Mr. Bennett's habitation to your father?" Conrad asked.

Jane wanted to know, too. Also, was it possible Ashley had worked with Tom in hopes of boosting her viewership? No. No, surely not.

"He pretended to be a live-in nurse. But I had no idea Tom was a person of interest in the murder of Josh Gunn."

Learning your former lover was not only a dirty rotten blackmailer but possibly a murderer must be a shock to the system.

"Do you know who might be supporting Mr. Bennett now?" Conrad asked, riding the same wavelength as Jane.

"No, but I caught him with a woman last week. He called me to the Lounge, and I went running because you do not tell Tom no. Jessica Thacker was leaving the break room, and she was ticked. She acted as if she'd been in there complaining about the service, but I knew better. I recognize the F-look when I see it. Fury, fear and frustration."

Yet another link to Jessica Thacker.

Barrow asked a few questions that led nowhere, then slid a pen and pad of paper over to Barbie, concluding the interview. "You know the drill. Write down everything you told me and any other details you recall."

Jane leaned against the wall to process everything she'd seen and heard.

What did all of this mean?

Who was guilty, who wasn't?

What did everything point to?

Thankfully, she knew her next move. The tour of Deputy Gunn's house.

CHAPTER TWELVE

Thou shall always be ready to break into a spontaneous song
or dance to entertain the crowds.

–Jane Ladling's Campaign Companion Code

onrad parked Jel in Deputy Gunn's driveway, next to Special Agent Barrow's GBH issued sedan. Jane drew in a deep breath, taking stock. Morning sunlight framed the house and really made the yellow crime scene tape across the front door pop. The neighborhood itself was quiet, only a dedicated fur-mom pushing a dog in a stroller.

That Jane was the consultant of an GBH consultant certainly had perks. During every other investigation, she'd had to sneak around to score a treat like this. Being able to walk right into an incident site was going to rock. However, they were near the worst spot of all time—Conrad's shooting. What if the shooter hid nearby, eager for a second try?

The future sheriff shut off the engine, clasped Jane's hand, and brought her knuckles to his mouth for a kiss. "What is going on inside that big, beautiful brain of yours?"

Jane tapped her temple. "Just pouring through what I've learned for each suspect and battling anxiety for your safety." Since leaving his house, she'd kept alert, searching for anyone skulking in bushes or tailing them. He'd refused to wear a bulletproof vest.

"Agents have been on patrol in the area all day."

That was something, at least. "Are you as confused by the evidence as I am? Nothing answers all our questions."

"That's how cases are sometimes."

"Well, I don't like it."

His lips twisted as he fought a grin.

Stop focusing on his mouth. "Tom is the most likely shooter. He's a liar and a blackmailer, and he had motive and opportunity. But why jeopardize his whole operation. Unless he panicked. If he killed Gunn, he has a lot to cover up."

"Barrow is convinced Bennett did committed both crimes, but without a confession, the case is wobbly at best. Too many unknown variables, with too much room for interpretation. According to Raymond, the prosecutor in this county resists trying a case with only circumstantial evidence. Which is why Barrow has agreed to let you tour the house. He thinks you may see something we missed."

"You can tell him it's okay to be impressed with my investigative skills and deductive reasoning," she teased, fluffing her hair. "Tell yourself while you're at it."

Conrad's warm chuckle thrilled her to her toes. Right on cue, Barrow emerged from his vehicle and motioned for Conrad, and only Conrad, to join him.

"Give me a minute." Her boyfriend kissed her cheek, released her hand and joined his buddy in the cold.

Remaining in the warmth of Jel, Jane withdrew her phone from her purse. Maybe she'd heard back from Ashley about the shooting. Oh! Texts from Fiona, Beau, Tiffany, June and yes, Ashley.

> NewsKat: I'll run a story as soon as Mr. Ryan gets me a quote.

Would he give one? A question for later. She checked the other messages, rather than respond. First, she needed to craft the perfect response.

> Fionality: How is our special agent boy today? Did you decide his V-day present? Because I have an idea that requires zero prep!!!!!!!!!!!!!

> Jane: He's better, and yes, yes, yes, please and thank you! Give me all the ideas!

> Fionality: I haven't gotten to see you enough lately, so I'm holding this idea hostage. Come over this evening and bring Tiff. We'll teach her how to sew funny bunnies and chat.

Fiona and Jane love to knit toys on lazy summer afternoons and freezing winter nights, then donate each piece to nearby children's charities.

> Jane: I'll be there with bells on. Not literally. And okay, okay, I'll bring Tiff. She's not terrible.

For some reason, the widow continued to grow on her.

Sighing, Jane checked the message from the cottage's newest guest.

> Tiffinator: I did rounds without being asked. I'm basically a superhero! Also, I miss Rolex. BRING HIM HOME!!!!

> Jane: Uh, superheroes wear capes. Everyone knows that.

Jane: I refuse to admit Rolex misses you too.

Jane: Fine! Maybe I'll bring him over and you can adore him before we visit Fiona. By the way, we're visiting Fiona tonight.

As Tiffany sent her roughly a thousand different heart emojis, Jane turned her attention to Beau's message.

Beaudyguard: I reached the bottom of the cesspool and discovered the first online mention of the Gentleman. A message from a terrified customer who'd just gotten a trim from Denise Allen.

Terrified, huh? Nothing Denise shared with Jane had been terrifying. What if the stylist shared more because she'd been tooting her own horn? For all Jane knew, Denise had dated "Joshie" to pilot his investigation, or even for grins and giggles, broke up with him when he got too close to the truth then let one of her minions take care of the problem. So... back to the hitman theory?

Jane: Could Denise be the Gentleman?

Beaudyguard: Honestly, I don't think there is a mob boss in AH.

Now there was an idea. Let's say her friend was right. His judgment was impeccable, his instincts spot on. So. If the Gentleman wasn't real, who had made him up and why?

Denise? Gunn himself, to create evidence against his enemies? Tom Bennett, to garner a deal with authorities? A *help them nail the top dog and let the little fish go free* situation. What about Madeline Gunn, to save the man she once believed she loved?

A line to explore after the tour. Finally, Jane switched her focus to the message from her sister.

> Juniverse: What are you doing next month?

In March? Why?

> Jane: Same as always. Taking care of the Garden. You?

No response. Jane sighed. Her younger sister lived close to their mom. The two were very similar, in fact. Sweet but flighty and very high energy. The few times they were together, Jane remembered being exhausted by the flurry of activity.

She glanced at Conrad. He and Barrow remained deep in conversation. Might as well handle Ashley. She knew what to say. Rather than reply to the text, Jane dialed the reporter's number.

"How's Mr. Ryan?" Ashley asked, in lieu of a greeting.

"He's good, thank you."

"I'm so glad." Relief coated the other woman's tone. "When I heard about the shooting on my scanner, I raced to the hospital to get the scoop. I was so shocked to see the paramedics wheel in Mr. Ryan." She laughed. "At this point, I might as well just call him Conrad."

Ah. A scanner. That explained how she'd known what happened. *Note to self: Buy a scanner.* The best part? Jane hadn't even needed to ask to gain an answer. But, though she waited, the reporter didn't launch into another story, answering Jane's other questions.

As innocently as possible, she tried stealthily maneuvering things in the direction she wished to go. "I'm so grateful you knew nobody else would call me."

To her surprise, Ashley snorted. "Okay. I know a leader when I hear one."

"Leader?" As in a monarch?

"A query meant to inspire me to talk. You suspect me of being involved somehow." Amusement saturated the words. "You're consistent, I'll give you that. Here's the story. I knew the guys weren't going to call you because I overheard them talking about it. Since you're working to find the person who threatened my life, I'm happy to help you any way I can." She released a frustrated noise. "Fine! I guess that means you can except a story without a quote. People need to know there's a shooter running around rather Conrad goes on record or not."

Dang it. No way the reporter had killed the deputy. She was a pretty okay person, and Jane was seriously growing to like her. Although, the last time she'd fallen into friendship with a suspect, she'd inadvertently helped a bank employee steal fifty thousand dollars.

She sighed. "Why couldn't you be a supervillain to my superhero?" Unlike Tiffany, Jane wore an invisible cape. The cloak of justice! "I think I was looking forward to having a worthy nemesis," she admitted.

Ashley laughed outright. "Maybe next time." Then her laughter sobered. "I have to ask. Did Conrad get a letter before the shooting?"

"No. He never did. I haven't either. Have you gotten a second?"

"Nope. According to my very handsome bodyguard, I haven't been followed, either. Nobody has stalked me through dark alleys, tried to break into my home, or planted a bomb under my car. I had Trick check. I even let him borrow the mirror with an articulated arm I ordered."

Hold up, that did sound cool. Conrad would adore it. Was it V-Day surprise perfect, though?

"Tom Cat Bennett. Allen. The Thackers. The Garfields. Unnamed mobsters." Ashley sighed. "Every lead has been both a dead end and a bridge to a thousand other possibilities. There's something off with this whole thing."

Jane smacked her palm on the dashboard in triumph. "Exactly what I said!" Though she might change her tune when she got her first full look at the crime scene. "The problem is, not a soul seems to know anything about the Gentleman or have firsthand experience working with him."

Should she test the waters of Beau's theory with Ashley? "Maybe there isn't a Gentleman," On a roll, Jane voiced other thoughts rapid-fire. "What if Deputy Gunn made him up? A reason to follow and harass Tom? Or maybe control Tom." Not even Sheriff Moore had trusted the man.

"Whoa there," Ashley said. "That's some imagination. I'm impressed."

Conrad nodded to his former partner, and the two men stepped apart. Staring at Jane, he headed her way.

"I've got to go," she told the reporter. "I'm about to tour the crime scene."

The other woman bellowed, "What! You can't make a statement like that without explaining—"

"Thanks for the tip," she interjected before hanging up.

Conrad opened the car door and helped her exit. Cold swamped her as they raced up the stairs, joining Barrow.

The agent captured her gaze. "Touch nothing, and only step where we step. Wear these just in case." He passed her a pair of latex gloves.

"I'll be good," she assured him, securing the protective covering in place.

Past the tape and through the foyer they went. A musty odor tainted the air. They stopped at the edge of the living room, giving Jane her first, err, second glimpse of the crime scene. She took in everything at once before concentrating

GENA SHOWALTER & JILL MONROE

on the finer details. The outline of the body. The broken mug. The thick black coffee dried on the wood floor planks.

Natural light slipped through slats int he metal blinds covering the windows. No curtains. No TV, but he had devoted a wall to a series of family photos. Across from that was a large bookshelf filled with forensic textbooks and dozens of mysteries. Everything from police procedurals to likable gumshoe private detective novels. Besides the side tables likely put together with instructions in an unknown language, there was a couch that looked brand new and a matching recliner more worn than a pair of cowboy boots at a Texas rodeo. Clearly the recliner was his favorite spot.

Jane tried to tune everything out. From her theories, to the two men beside her, to her natural curiosity. In that moment, she did her best to become Josh Gunn on an average Saturday morning. He'd been walking around, sipping his morning motor oil.

Barrow pointed to an area. "He fell here and banged his head against the coffee table there."

A variety of objects graced the coffee table. A collection of pens and unused notepads, plus scissors, a roll of tape, and empty candy and chip wrappers. There was a mug ring at the edge, where he'd forgotten to use a coaster.

Barrow whipped a stack of photos from his pocket. She recognized them as the crime scene pictures he'd shown her at the police station, plus extras he hadn't. "This is what covered the table before we took relevant items for testing."

She accepted the offering and flipped through the images. The cameraman had snapped various angles and distances of the room and even the files and letters, which were part of the things taken for testing. Jane launched a compare and contrast mission. Also missing was a small plastic baggie with a dusting of white powder and—

She gasped, saying, "There was a second mug." Her gaze flipped up to the agent. "Someone had coffee with him?"

"There was a second mug, yes, but it contained only Deputy Gunn's DNA and prints."

So he might have been drinking from both. Had he gotten a fresh cup when the first one went cold?

"Do you see anything that might lead to BOSS?" Barrow asked.

Jane spun in a slow circle, examining the most minute of details, thinking, thinking. If she were a deputy trying to solve a case and hide information from her coworkers, she would...

"May I sit on the recliner?" she asked. "To better get into character, I should experience what Gunn—Josh experienced. So where better to perch than his favorite spot? It will help me delve into the inner workings of his mind."

Barrow's head bobbed as if he were processing, then he nodded. "All right. After this, the scene is being released to the owner, so I don't see a reason to deny you."

Jane smoothed the skirt of her fit-and-flare and sat before he changed his mind. Once again, she scanned the room. Nothing out of the ordinary... Wait. There. The wall. The array of framed family photos. Each image contained either a picture of a happy couple, young and old, or kids playing with a dog. Something about those images...

Jane stood and closed the distance. Hey! These were the placeholders that had come with the frames. Each of those frames bore a scuff mark on the top, in the center, as if... Before she remembered to seek permission, she reached out and removed a frame from the wall, then turned it to examine its back. A piece of thin brown paper was taped over a lumpy back. A gentle tug caused a rip. Oops. Or rather, yay!

"Found it!" she exclaimed, removing the rest of the paper.

The guys rushed over, and she revealed what she'd discovered. A printed mugshot for Thomas Bennett, with multiple strings in a variety of colors taped around the edges. A puzzle!

Conrad confiscated another frame with gloved hands and ripped over the paper, revealing a printed headshot from the *Headliner* website featuring the smiling face of Ashley Katz and more strings.

Barrow reached out to do the same, but Jane stopped him, saying, "We don't want to screw up the order. Give me a few minutes, and I can tell you where each string is supposed to point and recreate the entire board." She rubbed her hands together. "Stand back and let me work."

To her surprise, they conceded after Conrad replaced the photo.

"Am I about to witness The Great Unraveled Raveling?" Barrow asked Conrad.

The what now?

"You are," her boyfriend replied, sounding amused and prideful.

Great Unraveled Raveling? What did that even mean?

No worries. "My Pops and I used to work puzzles together. Those with pieces, shapes, colors, numbers. You name it, we solved it. It's only a matter of figuring out what goes where without compromising other evidence." Once more, Jane tuned out the lawmen and their mysterious code talk, then removed the paper from each photo and and re-hung them in the proper direction. Using the size of each string as a key, she measured each possible connection. A job that required over an hour of intense concentration, all while Barrow snapped photos and video with his phone. Conrad wanted to help, but she insisted he rest and take notes. The man had been shot, for goodness sake.

When she finished, she studied Deputy Gunn's handi-

GRAVE WARS

work. Not bad. Not bad at all. Twelve photos in total. Three rows of four. Up top: Tom Bennett, Conrad, Jane, and a bowler hat adhered to a photo of someone who kind of resembled Thomas. The name written beneath read *Oliver Bennett* with a question mark at the end.

On the second row: Ashley, Hugh Garfield's children Barbie and Ken, and Hugh himself. On the final row: the mayor, Jessica, a faceless outline with a cut out of brown hair, and Denise Allen, the ex-girlfriend.

Most of the pictures had come from a driver's license, a database Gunn had mined for his own personal gain. Did the faceless outline represent the Gentleman? Or did that honor belong to the top hat wearing Oliver Bennett, whose driver's license photo that must have been issued several years after his death.

But that license hadn't bore the name Oliver Bennett. It couldn't. Otherwise Gunn wouldn't question his identity. So what name had the maybe living Oliver used?

Conrad and Barrow flanked her sides, studying the deputy's handiwork.

"What do the colors represent?" the special agent asked.

"I'm not sure—yet." Jane motioned to the photo of Tom's brother. "But we might have two Bennetts running around town."

CHAPTER THIRTEEN

Thou shall always be ready to provide a witty comeback for
every complaint or suspicion.

–Jane Ladling's Campaign Companion Code

*W*hile Conrad and the GBH team doubled their
efforts to hunt down the Bennett brothers
and unearth the mystery man, Jane picked up Rolex, then
Tiffany, and headed to Fiona's. Her thoughts refused to
settle.

Was Oliver alive? Was he the Gentleman? Had Jane
discarded every credible theory during her investigation to
pursue duds? Barrow considered the case solved. He believed
Thomas and Oliver worked together to kill Deputy Gunn,
who had discovered their secret. She didn't know what to
think anymore. Her gut remained silent.

And what about BOSS? What did those different colored
yarns mean? Green, as in monetary connection? Red might
point to passion and romance. There was a crimson string
linking Jane to Conrad, after all. Only, there was also a

crimson string connecting the brothers. So, a blood tie? Except, Jane and Conrad weren't related, thank goodness.

Maybe the colors meant nothing? Deputy Gunn could've used what he'd on hand, and they all represented the same thing. But why were there multiple strings connecting the same people, just in different colors?

Argh! Had anything ever been as frustrating as this case?

"Earth to Jane," Tiffany said from the passenger seat, petting Rolex as he soaked up the attention. "Okay if we finally go in?"

She blinked, the present world overtaking the mental one. Goodness gracious. How long had she sat behind the wheel of the hearse, parked in Fiona's driveway without uttering a word or moving a muscle?

"Yes, yes, of course," Jane rasped. "My apologies for the delay, baby."

"Oh, no need to apologize to me." Tiffany kissed the top of Rolex's head. "I'd wait forever to see Fiona."

Um... "I was obviously speaking only to Rolex."

"We both know that's not true," the widow replied primly. "Oh! Is it okay if I have Jessie over for breakfast tomorrow? She isn't mad at me anymore!"

"It wouldn't matter if she was." Why did Tiffany like such an uppity person? "She isn't a true friend. You know that, right?"

The widow gave Rolex another kiss. "I do know that, yes. But she's a power player in this town, and I need her on my side if I'm going to rise from the grave that has become my life and succeed."

"Well, making true friends might be a better place to start." What would Jane do without Conrad, Fiona and Beau?

"I hear you, okay? Now enough heavy stuff. Let's go enjoy the day."

They exited the vehicle, entering the cold. Fiona opened

up and welcomed them inside with a bright smile. They hugged and settled in the living room, where their amazing hostess had set up an array of delicious snacks, drinks and knitting supplies. Rolex plopped down between Jane and Tiffany's feet, as if he couldn't choose between them.

Was Jane being punished? Had she inadvertently insulted her precious fur-child? Forgotten third breakfast or fourth dinner too often?

"Eat up, ladies," Fiona said, motioning to the refreshments—mini quiches, pigs in a blanket, cucumber sandwiches, veggie spring rolls and meatballs. "First, we eat and chat about Jane's problem, then we focus on our task."

A groove formed between Tiff's brows. "What's Jane's problem?"

Might as well answer for herself. "Tomorrow is Valentine's Day, remember?" Cupid's Jubilee. Love Fest. The big V. "But I still haven't gotten Conrad anything."

"This again?" The widow groaned. "Get a trench coat, get naked, and get busy. Boom. Done. Problem solved. He'll be putty in your hands."

While Jane sputtered, Fiona laughed and clapped. "While that will be a magnificent birthday gift once they're married, it lacks something for a holiday that celebrates emotional commitment. No, Jane, Conrad means more to you than any other man, so perhaps give him the best gift you can."

The moisture in her mouth dried. "What do you mean?"

"What else?" Smiling sweetly, Fiona handed them both a sweet tea. "Your heart. Open it up to possibilities."

"Oh, Fiona," Tiffany said with a sigh. "That's all I've ever wanted anyone to give me. It's perfect. Absolutely perfect." A teasing light entered her eyes. "*If* Jane has an open heart to give."

Jane gulped. Perfect? Yes. But could she do it? Fiona

wasn't wrong. It could be the most important gift Jane had to offer. A true sacrifice of defenses, vulnerabilities, and fears.

Admitting to herself that she loved the man had taken months of mental and emotional gymnastics. A private gut-punch to the curse. Uttering the words aloud would intensify the battle. How could it not? Her relationship with the lawman was soaring to the next level.

But the man accepted the realities of the curse, and he deserved to hear how deeply her feelings ran. She shouldn't hide it. Hadn't her anger kindled when he'd stayed quiet about the shooting? The words she'd tossed his way resonated now more than ever: *You don't pick and choose what's good for me like I'm a child.*

Wasn't that what she'd done to him every time she'd broken up with him?

Yes, Conrad deserved better from her.

To her surprise, Tiffany reached over and patted her hand. "Look. That man adores you. It's clear to everyone who watches you guys interact. If you two can't make it, I might as well give up on finding happiness with a smoking hot curse breaker of my own."

How could Jane allow Tiffany to experience such a dismal fate? "I'll think about it," she rasped.

"Excellent." Fiona passed out plates.

Though her stomach was in knots, Jane selected a cucumber sandwich, a couple of meatballs, a veggie roll, and another three cucumber sandwiches. Her dear friend had worked hard to provide these snacks. No reason to waste them.

After she'd cleared her second plate, her cell phone rang, Conrad's face and name appearing on the screen.

Her heart started thudding. She left the girls laughing and stepped away to answer. "Hello Officer Inspector Detective

Special Agent Ryan." One of her favorite nicknames for him. "Is there something I can help you with?"

"There is indeed, pancake." One of his favorite nicknames for her, used only when he was in a top-notch mood and feeling extra affectionate. "Are you available to come to the station? I have news."

News? For the case? The holiday? What! She gulped. "What kind of news?"

He chuckled. "Come and see for yourself." Then the wretched, darling man did the unthinkable: he hung up on her.

Jane marched to her friends, explained what happened and, as they laughingly bid her goodbye, gathered her things. She made the drive to the station in record time without speeding. Much.

Conrad waited for her in the lobby. As soon as she entered, he strode over, smiling. Her heart thudded.

"What's going on?" she rasped.

His smile only widened as he clasped her upper arms. "I wanted to tell you in person. We've located Tom. A victim of his blackmail came forward and told us where he was hiding. Barrow arrested him and charged him with Deputy Gunn's murder. Additionally he's being questioned about the attempt on my life."

Different sounds left her. What! "That's amazing! Was Oliver found, too? And what is Barrow's smoking gun?" Before, the agent had insisted he needed stronger evidence.

"Thomas created a passport and driver's license for Oliver, intending to start over somewhere else using his brother's identity. He also had in his possession three small plastic packets of the same drug that killed the deputy, either to use or sell. Our current theory is that the deputy discovered his plan to disappear while investigating the Gentleman, who Thomas invented to stay out of prison. Moreover, Thomas possessed the same caliber of gun used to shoot me."

Wow, wow, wow. "Has Tom admitted to the crimes?" Was he, in fact, responsible? Or... Some of her excitement dimmed. Yeah. Or. This seemed perfectly right, but at the same time wholly wrong. Like a bow tied sloppily; it was done, but wasn't pretty. Or was she merely hoping the case continued, so she could work and live with Conrad a little longer? Because who else could the killer be? Jessica? Denise, as previously suspected? The mystery man?

"He hasn't confessed," Conrad said, and sighed.

"Where was he hiding?"

"You were right. We found him at another blackmail victim's home. A woman in Atlanta. He refuses to speak with anyone but his attorney. Barrow is certain he's the Gentleman and just as convinced we'll get a conviction."

"And you? What do you think?"

What *did* Jane herself think? The initial doubt was only growing. The completed puzzle just didn't seem to fit.

Conrad stretched his neck. "Barrow isn't wrong. We'll definitely get the conviction."

Had Conrad's tone flattened the slightest bit? Did he not believe Tom was responsible? She shrugged. "I guess the case is solved then?"

"Looks like," he said with a nod, his expression giving nothing away. "The threat of danger has ended."

Oh, yeah. A part of her had indeed hoped to stay with him longer. Because right now all she felt was disappointment. "There's no reason for me to spend another night at your place, I guess."

His features softened. "Sweetheart, there's always a reason for you to spend the night at my place."

Well. If he insisted she stay another night, she'd have to—

"But I do know you have duties at the Garden," he added, "and I won't stop you from seeing to them."

She slapped on what might be an overbright smile. "Yes. Of course."

An elevator dinged, and seconds later, Barrow rounded the corner, approaching with a file in hand. "Hate to interrupt, but we're ready for round two of questioning." He patted Conrad's shoulder, letting him know he was invited to participate, before he turned an apologetic eye to Jane. "I'm sorry, but the prosecutor is fully involved, and consultants of consultants are out. Conrad is an exception because the election for sheriff is a lock."

"Will you at least ask Tom why he never sent me a threatening letter?" she beseeched.

"If it comes up organically," the agent said, but Conrad winked at her, letting her know it was as good as done. When Barrow's phone dinged, he glanced at the screen and huffed. "Give me a minute." He stomped to a private corner to make a call.

Conrad kissed Jane's forehead. "I'll contact you when we finish up here. Tomorrow, I'll pick you up at six for your quote unquote best Valentine's Day ever."

She nibbled her bottom lip. "Yes, please reach out when you finish. But. Um. About tomorrow. Maybe we shouldn't give each other presents this year. Just this year. So there's no pressure. For you."

"Too late. I already got your gift." Mimicking a southern belle, he lurched back and pressed a hand over his heart. "Why, Jane Ladling-Ryan. Did you forget to buy or make your precious boyfriend a present?"

"How dare you?" she said with an affront she only halfway faked. "I absolutely did not forget. If anything, I over-remembered. Maybe I don't want you to feel inferior because my gift is so much better than yours. Huh? Did you ever consider that?"

"That's a trick question. There *isn't* a gift better than mine."

What! The pressure jumped to stage critical!

"Conrad," Barrow beckoned, waving him over.

Conrad kissed her brow. "See you tomorrow, sweetheart."

His voice was all calm—but she was all panic. "Sure, uh, thing."

* * * *

JANE WAS a bundle of nerves as she waited for Conrad to pick her up for their Valentine's Day date. He was late. Three minutes and forty-eight seconds late, to be exact. Had something bad happened?

"That dress is a dragon slayer," Tiffany said with a nod of approval.

They occupied the cottage living room, with Rolex curled up next to Jane, gazing adoringly at the widow. The crush had grown into a full-fledged obsession.

"Thank you." Despite the cold, she'd selected a summer fit-and-flare for the festivities. Pastel strips, exaggerated vee between the bust, and thin shoulder straps. Though she'd added her royal purple wrap coat. Might not fit the season, but it was a favorite dress, and she'd never worn it. What better day than Valentine's Day with her love? Rather than a hat, she wore a pink bow in her hair. "To be honest, I think I would prefer your outfit right now."

The widow managed to wow in an oversize T-shirt, ratty sweatpants and furry house slippers. Her dark locks were anchored in a messy bun. She lounged on the couch, balancing a carton of chocolate chip cookie dough ice cream on her stomach. The perfect style for a night of internal sleuthing. Exactly what Jane longed to do. Think.

Why did Tom take the time to invent the Gentleman but not plant better evidence? The supposed crime boss had slipped under local law enforcement's radar, as well as that of GBH agents, who'd probably scoured the town repeatedly since the murder.

Had Tom truly killed Deputy Gunn to protect his escape plan? If so, why had he picked a name linked to himself? The whole point of disappearing was, well, disappearing. Two and two weren't adding up to four. And if she was getting three, that meant Tom Cat might not be the killer.

So who was? And where was Conrad, anyway? He'd never been late.

"This Valentine's Day I'm dating myself, and I'm excited about it." Excitement crackled in Tiffany's eyes. "It was Rolex's idea, wasn't it, sugar?" She leaned over to pet him. "The sweetest little cookie suggested we celebrate all things me. I'm amazing, and it's time I realized it."

Jane tsked her tongue. "My darling little boy is determined to play near the wolf's den. I should probably shout *danger, danger,* but that will only send him deeper inside."

Rolex purred even louder, proclaiming his agreement.

Tiffany giggled, which caused Jane to giggle, and soon they were laughing together. Something akin to affection arced between them. A friends-for-life type of connection, and it sort of freaked her out.

She whipped out her phone, desperate for a distraction. Maybe she'd missed a message from Conrad. Nope. But she *had* missed texts from Beau and Ashley.

> Beaudyguard: I bought the murder house. The police released the scene, and the bank sold me the mortgage. When I flip it, I'll need an interior designer. You interested?

> Jane: Only if you're prepared to triple your investment! I'm THAT good.

> NewsKat: Thomas Bennett, huh?

Jane's heart leaped. She rushed to type:

> You have doubts?

> NewsKat: Many. Why go to so much effort to mail me a letter, then never even try to deliver on his threat, giving me the story of a lifetime?

> Jane: And why invent an alter ego to get yourself out of trouble, but stick around and not use the alias when you actually get in trouble? Although, there's an army of blackmail victims ready to do his dirty work. I imagine he's enjoying being exactly who he is too much.

Two hard raps sounded at the door, and Jane gasped. "He's here!" She dropped her phone in her purse, jumped to her feet, and smoothed her dress for the thousandth time. "I'm not sure when I'll be home," she told Tiffany, "but you have my number if anything happens. Don't hesitate to call me. I mean it."

Tiff rolled her eyes. "Get out of here already. You're ruining my date. The precious will be fine."

Jane draped her coat over her arm and approached the entrance. She inhaled and opened the door. Her pulse leaped. Conrad looked incredible. His hair was wonderfully wind-blown, his five o'clock shadow now a six o'clock storm cloud. An eggshell cashmere sweater stretched over his torso. Faded jeans encased his powerful legs. Leather loafers completed the casual sophistication.

Vulnerability washed over her in waves. What should she do, what should she do?

"I'm sorry I'm late. Something I was waiting on came in late and—" His gaze roved over her and heated. "You are heaven on earth, sweetheart."

Pleasure bloomed inside her. "You are forgiven. But, um, why are you so casual? You're the guy who wears a suit to converse with strangers."

"You'll see. It's a surprise." He smiled a bone-melting smile, then shifted and looked over her shoulder. "Hello, Tiffany. Rolex. She won't be back tonight."

She wouldn't? "Did Tom escape? Or has Barrow realized he hasn't yet solved the crime? Should I pack an overnight bag?"

Conrad helped her into a coat. "No, no and no." Irises twinkling, he offered her his hand.

What was he planning? And why hadn't he reacted to her hint that GBH might have screwed up?

Eyes wide, she accepted, twining her fingers with his. They headed to his black SUV, and he shut the door after seeing her safely into the passenger's side.

"Are you taking me to dinner?" she asked as he steered the car along back roads. "I think I remember an offer of a meal."

"You will eat, yes."

Wait. She recognized this route. "We're heading to your house."

He didn't confirm or deny but sure enough, in a matter of minutes they were parked at his bungalow. Grinning, he jogged around to open her door. Had he cooked her a special meal? What a sweet gesture. But if he hadn't included cinnamon sugar French toast, she might riot.

She cuddled into his side as they made their way to the

porch. Just past the door, she slapped a hand over her mouth. "You recreated the murder scene." He'd gathered coffee mugs, purple envelopes and folders and even taped an outline to present Deputy Gunn's body.

"I did. I also brought photos and old case files. Happy Valentine's Day, sweetheart. We will work this case until we're both satisfied with the end result."

He...this... With a broken cry, she threw herself against him. "I love you."

CHAPTER FOURTEEN

Thou shall always be ready to provide the perfect celebration for the big win. With you at his side, he can't lose.

–Jane Ladling's Campaign Companion Code

*J*ane breathed deep as the love of her life wrapped his strong arms around her and held on tight. As his heat and scent saturated her being, a dark cloud of fear evaporated. Suddenly she just knew. This was right. Tom absolutely was not the killer, and Conrad deserved her everything.

"You finally admitted you love me," he rasped, and she nodded. "Out loud."

"You already suspected?"

He eased back enough to cup her jaw. "Sweetheart, you trusted me with your cat. I suspected."

"By that logic, I love Tiffany, too," she grumbled, clasping his wrists.

The smile he gave her projected all kinds of warmth. "You do love Tiffany."

Hardly. Not Tiffany, the three-peat murder suspect and literal gold digger who was sometimes too snobby for her own good. "You can't know that."

"I majored in Jane Ladling. I know."

"I mean, I see why you might think so. We *do* share a great grandfather." And the widow *was* smart. And funny. And wounded. Also, they harbored the same hidden vulnerabilities.

Dang, Conrad had nailed it. She did. She loved Tiffany too. But whatever.

"There are worse things than falling in love with Tiffany Hotckins, I suppose." Jane gripped his shirt. "My heart is your Valentine gift, in case you didn't realize. If you're expecting anything else, you're not getting it."

With a chuckle, he leaned down and pressed his forehead against hers. As he traced the pads of his thumbs against her cheeks, he said, "Unfortunately, I can't give you my heart in return tonight, since you already own it. I love you, too, Jane Eleanor Ladling. Have since the moment I met you."

"I know," she croaked, pushing the admission past a lump in her throat. "You were helpless against my charms."

"As helpless as you were against my muscles."

She snorted, but he wasn't wrong. But now there was no going back. She'd voiced her feelings, poking and prodding at the curse, her biggest enemy. Whatever punches it threw next, she must remain strong.

"For the record, you were right. Your gift blew mine out of the water." Conrad kissed her lips once, twice, then straightened and released her. "Are you ready to prove or disprove the charge that Thomas Bennett killed Deputy Gunn and shot at me?"

"You mean the Case of the Officer and the Non-Gentleman? The Gentleman Who Preferred Cons? Cemetery Girl Buries A Gentleman?" Wow, her best titles yet. She was getting good at this. Though she longed to return to his embrace, she rubbed her hands together. First things first. "I'm more than ready." His life was at stake, and she wouldn't stop until she found the answers she sought.

"Good. Then get changed."

"Excuse me?"

"You're used to solving crime at a party while dressed up, yes? From ballgowns to eighties pop stars." He strode to the couch, where a stack of clothing waited. His clothing. A white T-shirt and gray sweatpants. The fluffy socks were new, however. As were the black slippers with cat faces. "This costume is called Pawvite Investigator Comfortable at Home," he told her with a wink.

"You rock so hard." Jane practically soared through the clouds as she made her way to the bathroom, where she donned the "uniform." As comfy, cozy as Tiffany now, she rejoined Conrad in the living room.

He pointed to an array of her favorite snacks and drinks on the sideboard in the dining room. "Cheddar is spending the night with Wyatt again, so you can put anything anywhere and it won't get shredded." He handed her Truth Be Told and a pen. "There's some good stuff waiting for your attention, including the police report from the car accident that took Oliver Bennett's life."

"Allegedly."

"What information wasn't available to the public, I recreated from memory." He gave her a mug with *Hers* scrawled across the center, then picked up a mug bearing the word *His*. "Hot chocolate for you, coffee for me."

"You thought of everything."

She sipped her drink as she studied photos and files, immersing herself in case details big and small. How much time passed, she didn't know. Didn't care. Well, she did care when she accidentally took a swig of Conrad's bitter black coffee rather than her decadently sweet hot chocolate. How he enjoyed motor oil, she would never know.

"What is this?" she asked, pointing to a paper with chicken scratch in the margins.

"A copy of a copy of a printout Deputy Gunn possessed. He copied it at work, took it home, and wrote notes we did our best to decipher." Her boyfriend tapped each hand-written section, explaining, "Because he suspected Oliver Bennett of being the Gentleman, Gunn noted ways the young man could have faked his death."

Hmm. The reasoning made sense, but only as long as Tom resurrected his brother to assume his identity. Still. Something niggled at the back of Jane's brain.

She set the page nearby and examined others. Reading. Thinking. Comparing.

Those two bullet holes in the deputy's wall. Tom had the gun, but had he made the shots?

What was with the hair? Who was that danged mystery brunette?

What did that top hat photo mean? On Deputy Gunn's makeshift murder board, Oliver Bennett was the only person with a symbol.

When Conrad wheeled out a surprise skein of yarn, a box of markers and a white board topped with a pink bow, she practically jumped up and down. This man checked all her boxes and lit all her wicks. After giving him a hug, she promptly went back to work.

As Jane meticulously arranged photos on the board, securing them with magnets, leaving notations along the way, she asked, "What do you think of Tom as a person?"

Conrad's expression turned thoughtful. "He's an extreme opportunist who uses people to get whatever he desires. His job put him in the path of wealthy socialites who unwittingly spilled family secrets while imbibing too much. But there's a big leap from skeeze to murderer. He had a good thing going. Why risk it?"

As usual, her boyfriend made total sense. "It feels as if we've got a suspect with motive and evidence, scant though it may be, but the bow on this present is crooked and the side of the box has dents." She stared at Tom's photo. "Everything is off."

"Bennett was a planner. Kept meticulous notes about his affairs for future blackmail opportunities. Took measures to ensure his safety, so his payees couldn't harm him. None of which we can prove because we have only the word of a couple ex-girlfriends. But I digress." He pointed to the photo of the crime scene. "The murder strikes me as sloppy. The evidence is garbled, pointing to too many individuals who've done nothing wrong. We are an example of that. Had Bennett planned it, he wouldn't be the primary suspect."

"That is an excellent point." She beamed at him. "Look at you, earning your detective's badge today."

He snorted.

"But," she added, "you never mentioned another suspect, which means you don't have one. Which means your badge gets taken away."

He pouted, and she laughed.

Back to the drawing board. Jane tossed out different theories, and Conrad always listened, asked questions and offered great feedback, even as evening turned into midnight and her thoughts began to scramble.

"Vampires," she piped up. "The deputy could have stumbled upon their existence, and they had to keep him quiet."

"Too much blood left inside his body and no puncture wounds."

"True." Her eyelids drooped, but she pushed through, continuing her investigation. Even when morning sunlight streamed through the windows. Again and again, her attention returned to the case file outlining the details of Oliver Bennett's fatal crash. Gunn had scrawled out dozens of handwritten notes:

- Real or Fake?
- Facial reconstruction surgery?
- Undocumented triplet?
- Identity theft?

He'd certainly possessed a vivid imagination. Jane approved. "If Oliver had reconstruction surgery, he could be anyone. Even Tom," she muttered.

"Maybe Tom was the one who'd died, allowing Oliver to take his place."

"But what would that mean for the murder investigation?" Something? Nothing?

"Okay, let's attack this another way," Conrad said. "Who is your top-of-the-line prime suspect?"

Yes, who *did* she believe was responsible? "The Tom Cat, after all?" Oh! New name alert. The Case of the Purrfect Murder. "What if he did the planning, but not the executing? His chosen blackmail victims are married women desperate to keep their extramarital affairs secret. All he had to do was snap his fingers, and a former lover do the dirty work for him. Maybe this woman wanted the law to find out about Tom, so she left clues?" Jane bounced on the balls of her feet as she warmed up to the idea. Then her shoulders rolled in. "But no. There's too much risk in involving a third party who hates you."

An ache registered in her back, and she rubbed her tense muscles. A yawn nearly cracked her jaw, fatigue washing over her. Oh wow. Her eyelids felt as if a thin layer of sandpaper had adhered to the inside.

"Why don't we take a quick nap and recharge?" Conrad suggested.

Her gaze returned to the accident report with the deputy's notes. "Not yet. I'm on the cusp of something, I think." She swiped up a photo and sank to the floor to sit cross-legged. "Was something in this empty baggie?" She pointed to the small, clear plastic with a dusting of white.

"Yes. The drug that ended up in his coffee."

"So the killer just left it there? Without fingerprints?"

"The deputy's prints were on it, along with prints too smudged to use. And yes, the killer left it behind. It could have fallen out of his pocket. Or hers. I'm not discounting your lover used for murder scenario."

She read over the deputy's notes again, both typed and chicken scratch. When she finished, she moved on to the accident, then his bid for Sheriff. He'd compiled a pretty hefty campaign file. But her gaze kept returning to the accident tidbit.

—*When asked what happened, the driver said nothing. I said you're sure, and he said no thank you. Obvious confusion and trauma.*

She zeroed in on one phrase in particular. *I said you're sure. I said you're sure.*

I said you're sure.

She took a closer look. Oh! "Your" sure, not "you're" sure. He'd made the same mistake there, there and there. Her brain must have subconsciously corrected his grammar. It was the same mistake the Gentleman had made.

Her eyes widened, a bomb of light exploding inside her. Of course! When you had the right pieces, everything fit. The puzzle put itself together. The who, the what and the why.

"You did it," Conrad said with a grin.

"I did! I really did." Jane threw her arms around him and settled in his lap right there on the floor.

"Tell me what you got."

"Deputy Gunn wanted to be sheriff. He must have thought he had it in the bag until Sheriff Moore endorsed you. For the first time, he realized he might lose this thing. When Ashley Katz ran that article featuring his fabrication of evidence, he probably had to speed up his timeline, bringing the crime boss into the spotlight sooner rather than later. *He* sent those threatening letters to himself," she announced, and her gut chimed in with a resounding *Yes!* Better late than never, she supposed. "The mistake between *your* and the *you are* contraction gave it away."

"Who knew grammar was such a double-edged sword?"

"No doubt the deputy hoped those warning letters would give credence to the mobster he'd invented. He probably expected Ashley Katz to jump at the chance to report on the scourge plaguing the good people of Aurelian Hills, and when she didn't, he had to up his game. That meant actually producing the crime boss. Enter Tom Bennett, the Casanova gigolo romancing Gunn's daughter."

One of Conrad's brows ascended in a show of curiosity. "Casanova gigolo?"

"Just go with it," she said, on a roll. "Maybe Deputy Gunn took drugs from his daughter and planted them on Tom, maybe Tom already had them. Either way, the deputy seized the chance to arrest the guy, giving him the perfect opportunity to negotiate terms. Pretend to work for the made-up Gentleman or go to prison. But Deputy Gunn intended to betray Tom all along and transform *him* into the mobster. How better to win the election than to bust a dangerous, up-and-coming crime boss?"

Conrad turned thoughtful. "So Tom figured out his plan and killed him? Or had him killed."

Here's where things got interesting. She shook her head. "You saw how cocky the bartender is, not to mention his incredible acting chops. He played the upset victim who'd never heard of the Gentleman to perfection. I doubt Tom was threatened by Deputy Gunn. Both Madeline and Tom mentioned the deputy doing something kind in Tom's past. I bet Deputy Gunn helped Tom the night his brother perished in that car accident. He had no desire to harm the man, especially irrevocably. And, with his illicit connections and a computer full of blackmail fodder, he was confident he could beat any charge Gunn lobbed at him."

"This is making sense. Go on."

"Gunn was in too deep to let Tom live. He may have even convinced himself he was doing the world a favor by getting rid of a man known for blackmailing—who might be blackmailing his own daughter." Jane stretched to grab a photo of the gunshots in the deputy's wall. "Plus, this element of the case has been bothering me. What if Gunn made it look as though an altercation occurred, hoping to kill Tom and claim it was self-defense?"

Conrad set her aside and surged to his feet to pace. A sure sign he was following her twisty mental pathway. "So how did Gunn die?"

"I think, well, he drugged himself. Accidentally. Or on purpose. No, accidentally." She nodded to let him know she'd chosen a final answer.

He blinked at her. "I'm going to need you to explain this one, Jane."

Happy to. "Gunn understood he had to get rid of the only person with knowledge of the Gentleman's inauthenticity, but realized he might not beat Tom in a fight. He chose the next best thing. Kill the supposed crime boss with an overdose."

"And the best vehicle for doing so was his morning coffee?" Conrad finished for her.

She grinned. "Look at that. You got it in one. I may have to return that detective's badge to you."

"And I'll cherish it. But I still don't understand how Gunn accidentally consumed the drug."

Easy. "Since he'd worked in law enforcement, he'd witnessed mistakes made by other criminals. To concoct a foolproof scheme, he just needed to do a test run to find out how the drug reacted to coffee. How the beverage looked and smelled. I think he poured himself a mug, plus a second to practice. Something could have distracted him, or maybe he'd been ultra-focused on another part of his scheme. Either way, he forgot there was a second mug."

"And without thought, he grabbed a mug and drank out of habit."

"Exactly." She nodded for emphasis. "He planted evidence in the wrong field and reaped a killer crop."

"But who shot me? Who sent Ashley Katz the letter?"

"I'm willing to bet Gunn mailed Ashley the letter right before his death, hoping to scare her into retracting her story and relaunching his campaign."

"Makes sense. The random strands of hair he swiped from his ex-girlfriend's salon were probably meant to be used as evidence at the Gentleman's crime scenes. Either to add a layer of intrigue, distracting the police and forensics team as they chased a red herring, or incriminate people who'd gotten on Gunn's bad side."

"Or both," Jane said. "As for your shooter, my money is on Tom. You are a lawman he can't buy or blackmail, and you found him at Hugh's house. He panicked." And now, with the truth known and Tom locked away, the future sheriff was safe. All was right in Jane's world.

Just like that, satisfaction was achieved. Case closed. Suddenly fatigue poured through her, and she yawned. "Well, time for sleepy night-night...in the early morning."

Conrad chuckled softly. "I need to speak with Barrow. I'm going to brush my teeth and go. Feel free to stay here as long as you wish. My home is your home."

She murmured her agreement, her heavy eyelids already closing. "Maybe I'll grab a short wee little nap."

"Good idea." The wonderful man swept her into his arms. "Couch or bed?"

"Bed please."

His chest puffed with something akin to contentment as he carried her to the main bedroom. A mattress cushioned her as he gently laid her down. Excellent. The softness reached her preferred firmness level: clouds.

He kissed her brow, whispering, "I'll return as quickly as humanly possible." Clothing rustled, and a door snicked closed.

Jane drifted off...until a cold hand clutched her arm and shook her.

"Ms. Ladling. Jane. Wake up."

What the—she blinked open her eyes and gasped. Jessica Thacker stood at the side of the bed, pale and trembling. She held a gun.

Jane jolted upright. "What are you doing? Why are you here? Why are you pointing a gun at me?"

The first lady licked her lips. "You will pick up your cell phone and call Mr. Ryan. You will tell him to release Tom, or I will kill you."

CHAPTER FIFTEEN

Thou shall remember that behind every great politician, there's an unsung heroine of style and snack management.

–Jane Ladling's Campaign Companion Code

*F*ully awake, Jane gawked at the intruder. Jessica's usually perfectly coiffed hair hung to her shoulders in utter dishevelment. A heavy, angry flush painted her cheeks in an uneven, mottled hue. Tear marks streaked her once flawless, subtle makeup. Her silk blouse was rumpled, her wool pants wrinkled. Gone was her poise and grace, replaced by vulnerability and desperation.

The mayor's wife backed away, but maintained her aim. "Grab the phone. Slowly."

"How did you get in? Why are you doing this?" Her heart raced, and her stomach twisted. Nerve endings hummed with apprehension as she reached for her cell phone. "What do you hope to gain by this?"

"Hurry!" Jessica snapped, ignoring her questions. The gun shook in her grip.

"I can't go slow and hurry at the same time." Jane considered her options. During their first case, Conrad had given her self-defense lessons. Should she risk going for the weapon? Toss a pillow in her attacker's face and run? Push for answers?

"Slow," the other woman grated.

At a pace a snail would envy, Jane clasped the phone and stood. Push for answers won. "You won't shoot me, Jessie." Establish a connection–check. Now, to be both firm and friendly, showing refusal to back down, but it was okay because they'd both benefit from it. "You need me to make the call. I'm happy to do it, but only after I know what's going on. Tell me why you're doing this. You weren't considered a person of interest any longer." Mostly. "You were free and clear."

Jessica scowled at her. "No one is ever free after meeting Thomas Bennett." She tossed an expectant look over her shoulder, as if searching for something. Whatever she saw calmed her, and she smiled. "But we will be."

Jane blinked. "We?"

"Hello, Cemetery Girl." A sweet-faced Tiffany entered the room and waved. "I hope you don't mind, but I used the guest facilities."

What! Betrayal? From Tiffany? No. No, no, no. Not her, the one Rolex so stalwartly adored. "How could you do this?"

Tiffany only had eyes for Jessica. Frowning, she pushed the first lady's hand down, lowering the barrel of the gun. "I told you a weapon wouldn't be needed."

Stubborn as a mule, Jessica aimed at Jane once more.

The widow exhaled heavily, then shrugged. "I'm sure you're wondering what's going on, Jane. Well, I'll tell you. Jessie came for breakfast this morning. We discussed our mutual Tom problem. She had a solution, so I signed on to

Team Freedom and gave her Conrad's spare key. It's helpful when you label things."

"I thought we had a friends-for-life moment," Jane said, pressing her palms against her stomach to calm the sudden flight of butterflies.

"Don't be ridiculous. Friends? You and me?" Tiffany scoffed. "I'm tired of being blackmailed, and I'm finally going to do something about it. Do you know how horrified I'd be if Tom posted videos of our private moments?"

Jane gnashed her teeth. "You told me you two only kissed."

"Stop acting like a child. I lied," the widow said, tossing her arms up. "Obviously."

Yes, but how could Tiffany do this? How could she threaten another life? Rolex loved and respected her. "Rolex may never forgive you for this."

"He's a cat. I'll get over it," she responded dryly, the final nail in her coffin.

"You are dead to me," Jane snapped, "and not in a good way."

"None of this was supposed to happen," Jessica cried. "For eleven months, I've met each of Tom's demands. I was saving to buy him off, but noooo. The deputy had to go and die, bringing the authorities onto the scene." Once she started talking, she erupted with information, unable to hold back her stream of grievances. "When the investigation into Josh's murder heated up, Tom vowed to blast footage of us if ever he landed behind bars."

"That must have sucked for you," Jane said with genuine sympathy. ,

"You have no idea the burden I've carried. The weight of it." Agony etched the older woman's features. "Tom set up new protocols to make sure I complied. If he fails to sign in to his laptop once a day, our private moments will automatically be emailed to my children and released onto the *Headliner*. I won't allow my mistakes to become public fodder. Nor will Tiffany." She drew in a sharp breath. Her expression hardened. "We have less than two hours until his next check in. That is why we're forcing your boyfriend to let Tom go. Call him and tell him you'll die if he doesn't."

Jane gaped at her. "Conrad could go to jail for something like that." As soon as she spoke, realization dawned. This was the curse in action. The knockout punch meant to forever remove the lawman from her orbit.

"That is a Conrad problem," Jessica quipped. "Call him."

"No," Jane grated. "No doubt you'll shoot me the moment the call ends. Besides, Conrad is merely a consultant on the case. He can't break a prisoner out of jail with only two hours' notice. He needs a full business day."

Tiffany snapped her fingers. "While Conrad's working, we should make Beau hunt for the footage. He's a computer wizard, and he'll do anything to save Jane. If anyone can find and delete old videos, it's him."

Hope sparked in Jessica's eyes but quickly died. "What if he doesn't delete it? What if he uses it the same way Tom does? A likely scenario, considering I'm holding a gun on one of his closest friends. No. We can't let anyone else access the footage. Jane, you'll call your boyfriend as ordered and tell him to facilitate Tom's release, either officially or unofficially, I don't care which. He may be a consultant, but he runs in and out of Aurelian Hills's police station like it's a drive-thru."

"She isn't wrong, you know," Tiffany said.

Jessica's face softened, as if she saw the end of the tunnel and only needed to sweeten the deal. "If Mr. Ryan does this, I'll ensure he becomes sheriff. I can do it. Then we can all get something we want and return to our normal lives like nothing happened." Her eyes narrowed to slits. "But understand this. If those videos get released, I'll kill your boyfriend and your cat and make you watch. Do you understand? Believe me, I'm not afraid to use this gun. I've done it before."

And that's when Jane knew Mrs. Thacker had been at Mr. Garfield's house with Tom. She shot Conrad. Had she also dressed as Tom to frame him?

Now it was Jane's turn to narrow her eyes. No doubt her expression conveyed only steely malice. The other woman's plan was decent, but it had a devastatingly fatal flaw—threatening Conrad and Rolex.

This. Woman. Must. Pay.

"You were with Tom at Mr. Garfield's. But you are who shot Conrad." Though her knees knocked, Jane raised her chin. "I won't do anything you ask."

Tiffany nodded her head with gusto and mouthed, "Trust me. Do it."

Jane frowned. Trust the traitor who was no doubt attempting to fool her again? No. Never! Except, Rolex did love her. And there was no living being more perceptive than Rolex the Grasshopper Slayer. So, maybe Jane should perhaps trust the widow?

Tiff had been so happy about her planned breakfast with the first lady. If Jessica had shown up and threatened Tiffany and/or Rolex, the widow would've agreed with anything to keep herself and the world's greatest treasure safe. So. Trust her? Yes. Jane was ready to take that step.

Jessica put both hands on the gun to steady her aim, desperation filling her dark eyes. "I meant what I said. If he comes through, we will all walk away with what we want. Nobody gets hurt, and we continue on with our lives like nothing happened. Now, enough stalling. Call him."

Oh, how mistaken the woman was. Neither Jane nor Conrad would rest until justice was served.

"All right, fine," Jane said. "I'll do it." She peered down at the phone and spied a text from June and Fiona on the screen.

> Juniverse: I'm coming to visit you next month. See you soon!

What the—

> Fionality: Something weird is going on. Raymond received a message from Conrad and flew out of my house!

Uh. Did they know about Jessica? Had Tiff, maybe, warned them?

"Go on," Jessica snapped. "Dial. And put it on speaker."

Reeling, Jane keyed up Conrad's number. The ensuing ring broke through the veil of silence cloaking the bedroom.

"Hello, pancake," he answered, sounding winded. Was he running?

Her chest tightened. "Hello, Inspector Detective Special Agent Ryan. I, um, need to speak with you." Her gaze darted to Jessica, who nodded. "It's important. Life and death, really."

"Before you say anything," Conrad interjected, "I need you to listen to me, okay? On my signal, hit the floor."

Jane's gaze widened as the first lady burst out, "What are you—"

"Now!" Conrad shouted.

A loud bang filled the house, causing Jessica to jolt.

"Hi-yah," Tiffany said, kicking the gun out of the other woman's hands. The weapon went flying and landed with a thud.

Jane dove for the piece, snatching it up while Tiffany followed her masterful kick with a sucker punch to the face. Aurelian Hill's first lady went down as Jane stood and aimed the gun at her.

"Don't you dare move a muscle," she snapped. "I'm placing you under citizen's arrest for threatening and endangering others, lying, nearly leaving Rolex motherless, breaking and entering with a key, and almost ruining the best Valentine's Day experience of my life."

"Did you see me?" Tiffany exclaimed, shaking her fist in the air. "I nailed that! Nailed it!"

"Now would be a good time to explain what's going on," Jane prompted.

The widow got serious in a hurry. "Jessie showed up for breakfast as planned only to pull that gun on me. She threatened to kill me to get to you. To buy time, I told her I had Conrad's key and a thirst for revenge too. I hoped my secret call to Conrad would help the cops beat us to the residence, but no. I had to buy more time by requesting a potty break for number two. Number two, Jane." Red infused her cheeks. "Thankfully, she fell for it. And so did you. I thought for sure you'd catch on when I said I didn't care if Rolex forgave me or not. As if I'd ever endure such a travesty!"

"I did catch on." Eventually. Jane smiled from ear to ear. "I was right about almost everything. I am the world's best crime solver!"

"And I am practically a superhero!" Tiffany smiled from ear to ear too. "You never answered my question. Did you see me? Huh, huh? Did you see what I did?"

"You were pretty good, I gu–" Jane stopped herself. Tiffany deserved to bask in the moment. "Actually, you were great. Amazing even."

Suddenly, Conrad, GBH agents, Beau and their buds rushed into the room. The future sheriff scanned the room until finding Jane. He raced over, claimed the gun and yanked her into his arms. He held her tight.

"You're all right, you're all right, you're all right," he chanted.

"I am," she promised. "Not a scratch, thanks to Tiff."

He paused long enough to frown at Tiffany. "You were supposed to duck, too, not execute a roundhouse kick."

The superhero simply shrugged. "I've been taking online classes to distract myself from the fact that I'm living in a cemetery with dead bodies. Pottery. Knitting. Even self-defense. It's amazing what you can do virtually these days. Anyway, I saw the opportunity and went for it. I must say, feeling my foot make contact with her hand was a rush I'll never forget."

The teeniest, tiniest flame of envy slithered through Jane. She'd never gotten to roundhouse kick a criminal. Yet.

But all that emotion faded when Sheriff Moore slapped cuffs on Jessica's wrists and listed her rights. Beau and Trick checked on Tiffany, who still beamed and kept asking, "Did you see it? Through the window, did you see it?"

"How did you know what was going on?" Jane asked her boyfriend.

"Tiffany activated her phone's speaker on the ride from the Garden. Thacker never noticed."

"And my quick thinking and bravery?" Jane may not have shown off her spinning kick skills, but she *had* faced down her would be killer without flinching.

Conrad shuddered, even as he grumbled, "You were perfect."

And look? The curse didn't take Conrad away from her. She fought and defeated it. Which was even better than a roundhouse kick. Almost.

The Sheriff walked Jessica out of the bedroom. The other woman's head hung low, defeat a heavy mask on her face. For a moment, Jane could spare the victim of blackmail a smidgeon of sympathy. After all, Jessica had been duped by a man who'd only used her.

Oh, wait a minute. Jane just remembered something. "Jessica is the one who shot you." Any sympathy dried up. "She was in the Garfield house with Tom when you showed up. I don't know how everything went down, but she confessed, and I'm willing to testify in court."

Outside the window, Sheriff Moore helped Jessica into the backseat of his squad car.

Conrad's head tilted. "GBH found some footage made by the bartender and evidence of the blackmail. He'll be going to prison too, his victims finally free. Though their lives might never be the same. There's a good chance their cheating will be revealed during the trial."

That was okay with Jane. Truth was better than lies any day of the week. But she hated the thought of anyone suffering a second longer because of the bartender's greed.

Justice was served.

"There's more," Conrad said. "Bennett kept a log of his blackmail, as well as Gunn's. Barrow found it and has barely scratched the surface, but it's already provided details we were missing."

"Do tell."

"Bennett knew about the deputy's plan to introduce the made-up mobster to the town. Gunn attempted to blackmail him into corroborating the claim that Bennett was his CI. A move meant to keep Sheriff Moore off his back and get the ball rolling on the investigation into the mysterious Gentleman."

So, there definitely wasn't a criminal underbelly attempting to wreak havoc in Aurelian Hills. Thank goodness!

"Bennett claims the deputy took the drugs from his daughter and tricked him into handling the baggies, thereby covering each with his fingerprints. That's why he engineered a way to enter Gunn's home. To seize the narcotics himself. We're working to verify his tale, but several elements of his story already check out."

Of course! She should have guessed. "Did he say anything about the bullet holes in the wall?"

"Gunn did it as part of his frame job."

A suspicion she'd once entertained. "I must say, I'm glad to have official answers."

Barrow took Jane's statement, then Conrad's, yet another hour passed before everyone cleared out of the bungalow. Only Beau, Trick and Tiffany remained.

Beau looked out the blinds. "That reporter, Ashley Katz, is on the front lawn, trying to interview Barrow."

"Maybe I'll give her an exclusive," Jane said, thinking out loud. "Oh! I owe Fiona an explanation." She whipped out her phone and texted her best friend in the world.

> Jane: I have so much to tell you! We caught the bad guy—and the bad girl. Everyone is safe. I'll come over tomorrow and fill you in (well, I'll fill in the details the sheriff leaves off because men.) I'll bring Tiffany (she helped!)

A response came only a few moments later.

> Fionality: Yes! I demand every detail. Come over anytime, the earlier the better! I love you, Jay Bird. With all my heart.

> Jane: I love you, too, Fee. With all my heart and soul.

"Oh!" Jane exclaimed, seeing her sister's name and remembering The Text. "My sister is coming to visit me next month."

"Is that dread I detect in your tone?" Conrad asked with a laugh.

"No! And yes. But mostly yes. She's a handful."

"Then I'm looking forward to meeting her." To everyone else, he called, "All right, time to go."

Beau and Trick snickered at him.

Tiffany yawned. "Can someone drive me back to the cottage?"

"We will," Trick volunteered.

"We'll be directly behind you," Conrad said, surprising Jane. He gave her a soft smile. "I'm a hundred percent certain you want to get your eyes on Rolex ASAP."

He knew her so well. "I really do." What a day this had been. They'd gotten a happy ending with the case. But. Tears welled, blurring her vision. She could've died today. She would have lost Conrad and Rolex, Fiona and Beau, Tiffany and the cottage. This bungalow. Not to mention the dream she hadn't admitted she harbored—until just this moment.

"Jane?" Conrad said, probably confused by her demeanor. "Get out faster," he called to the others, shooing them out. Their snickering continued until he shut the door. He drew Jane against his chest, rested his chin on the top of her head and petted her hair while she clung to him. "What's on your mind, love?"

"None of us are guaranteed a tomorrow."

"No. We're not." He offered no more.

How to explain the things swirling in her heart? "What we compromise to keep, we will eventually lose."

He went still for a moment. "What are you saying?"

"For too long, I've allowed the curse to dictate my decisions. I compromised my deepest desires to steal a taste of happiness with the world's most incredible man. But I don't want to compromise anymore."

Cupping her cheeks, he tilted her head until her gaze met his. "If you're attempting to break up with me, it's not gonna stick. We're together."

"I'm not attempting to break up with you," she replied with a soft smile.

Jane peered up at the man she loved more than life. Adoration and affection flooded her.

At the same time, confidence went to war with fear, her heart racing. She drew in a deep breath and finally uttered the words that would forever change her future. "Conrad Hotness Ryan. Will you marry me?"

* * * *

Look for *Grave New World* - the exciting conclusion to the Jane Ladling Mystery Series. Coming Soon.

* * * *

You can hang out with Gena and Jill on their Patreon where they share exclusive content.

* * * *

Books in the Jane Ladling Series
Romancing the Gravestone
No Gravestone Left Unturned
Game of Gravestones
Twelve Graves of Christmas
Conrad: Falling For the Gravekeeper
Grave Wars

* * * *

Books in the Writing Fiction Series:

All Write Already

All Write Already Workbook

The Write Life

Write Now! An All Write Already Journal

ABOUT GENA SHOWALTER

Gena Showalter is the New York Times and USA TODAY bestselling author of multiple "unputdownable" series in paranormal, contemporary, and young adult romance.

Learn more about Gena, her menagerie of rescue dogs, and all her upcoming books at genashowalter.com

ALSO BY GENA SHOWALTER

Immortal Enemies

Start with: Heartless

·

Rise of the Warlords

Start with: The Warlord

·

Lords of the Underworld

Start with: The Darkest Night

·

White Rabbit Chronicles

Start with: Alice in Zombieland

·

Tales of an Extraordinary Girl

Start with: Playing with Fire

·

Everlife

Start with: Firstlife

·

Original Heartbreakers

Start with: The Secret Fling

·

Angels of the Dark:

Start with: Wicked Nights

·

Otherworld Assassins

Start with: Last Kiss Goodnight

.

Gena's Complete List of Releases:

GenaShowalter.com/books

ABOUT JILL MONROE

Jill Monroe is the international best selling author of over fifteen novels and novellas. Her books are available across the globe and ***The Wrong Bed: Naked Pursuit*** has been adapted for the small screen for Lifetime Movie Network.

When not writing, Jill makes her home in Oklahoma with her husband, enjoys daily walks with her dog Zoey, texting with her two daughters and collecting fabric for items she'll sew poorly.

Learn more about Jill at jillmonroe.com

ALSO BY JILL MONROE

Sworn Series:

Sworn Promises

Sworn Duty

Sworn By A Kiss

Sworn Protector

Sworn Enemies

Sworn Instinct

.

Wrong Bed Series

Naked Thrill

Naked Pursuit*

*(Now a movie from Lifetime Movie Network)

.

From Hallmark:

At The Heart of Christmas

.

Spicy Romance:

Fun & Games

Treasure in the Sand (novella)

.

Jill's Complete List of Releases:

https://jillmonroe.com/allbooks/

Made in United States
North Haven, CT
25 September 2023